MW00878688

SURVIVING

AUNT MARSHA

SOFIE LAGUNA

SCHOLASTIC PRESS ▪ NEW YORK

Copyright © 2004 by Sofie Laguna. All rights reserved. Published by Scholastic Press, an imprint of Scholastic Inc., *Publishers since 1920,* by arrangement with Omnibus Books, an imprint of Scholastic Australia Pty Ltd. SCHOLASTIC, SCHOLASTIC PRESS, and associated logos are trademarks and/or registered trademarks of Scholastic Inc.

No part of this publication may be reproduced, stored in a retrieval system, or transmitted in any form or by any means, electronic, mechanical, photocopying, recording, or otherwise, without written permission of the publisher. For information regarding permission, write to Omnibus Books, 52 Fullarton Road, Norwood SA 5067.

Library of Congress Cataloging-in-Publication Data

Laguna, Sofie, 1968–
Surviving Aunt Marsha / Sofie Laguna.—1st American ed.
p.   cm.
Summary: When Mum and Dad go on a much-needed vacation to "find their lost romance," three Australian siblings are forced to spend three weeks with their least favorite aunt.
ISBN 0-439-64485-2
[1. Aunts—Fiction. 2. Brothers and sisters—Fiction. 3. Australia—Fiction.] I. Title.
PZ7.L144Su 2005
[Fic]—dc22
2003067346

10 9 8 7 6 5 4 3 2 1   05 06 07 08 09
Printed in the U.S.A.   37

The text type was set in 13-point Perpetua.
Book design by Kristina Albertson

First American edition, February 2005

FOR
STEFAN,
INGRID,
AND
ALEX

BAD NEWS

IT WAS BREAKFAST AT 1 MACLUSKY STREET. DAD WAS BOILING eggs and making toast, Mum was drinking tea and making sure Dad didn't burn the toast, Vince was feeding toast crusts to Mandy, our dog, and Aidan was reading *Phantom and the Amazons* and singing "Unchain My Heart" along with the radio. I was busy noticing everything. I'm Bettina, but everyone calls me Tina, or Tine. I'm eleven — twelve in three months — and I'm a big noticer.

"Kids," said Dad, sounding nervous, "your mother and I are going on our winter vacation, as you know, and this time — well, we're going to be gone for a bit longer than usual. We want to — we're going for — for, we want to go for three weeks. We want to go to Paris and — well — we've asked your Aunt Marsha to come and stay with you and — the good news is that she's said yes, that she'd love to —"

"Noooo!" We interrupted him with our three-at-once groan.

"And this time" — Mum looked at us hard with her eyebrows raised up — "you are going to make your Aunt Marsha feel welcome."

AUNT MARSHA'S WAY

MUM THOUGHT AUNT MARSHA'S WAY OF DOING THINGS was the right way even though Mum never did things the way Aunt Marsha did. Mum was messy. She says she inherited the messy gene from her dad and that no matter what she did, everything around her turned into a mess. Dishes piled up in the sink, beds unmade themselves, and dirty clothes spread out over the laundry room floor as soon as she walked into the house. She said she was cursed and that there was no point in fighting it. That's why our house was so messy.

We liked our mum the way she was, but Mum said she really should be tidier and more organized like Aunt

Marsha. She said a dose of Aunt Marsha would probably do us good.

Sometimes at Christmas or Easter Aunt Marsha came to stay with us and she always tidied up the whole house, even if it was full of people. Maybe Aunt Marsha had inherited the *tidy* gene from *her* dad. She scrubbed the black bits off the pots and pans and stacked them in neat piles, she dusted the photos in frames and the vases and the paintings on the walls, and she lined up all the herbs and spices and breakfast cereals and tin cans in tidy rows in alphabetical order. Suddenly everything in the house was *ABC*. Dad said he could never find anything.

"Sandy (that's my mum), do you know where the Vegemite is?" Dad would call out, his head in the cupboard.

"Well, Vegemite starts with a *V*, which comes after *U*, so it must be next to something in the cupboard starting with a *U*!"

"But nothing in the cupboard starts with a *U*!"

"What about *onions*?" Vince would yell from the telly room.

"*Onions* is with an *O*!" Dad would yell back. "Bloody Marsha!"

After Aunt Marsha had been to stay, Mum said we should

invite Mr. Meldine, the school principal, over for dinner because the house looked like a house she could be proud of. Aunt Marsha used to be a nurse and Mum loved that, too. She used to be the boss of the whole children's ward at the Royal Canberra Hospital, and Mum said she could relax if Aidan fell out of a tree or if Vince stuck a five-cent coin up his nose because we'd be in the hands of a professional.

Dad, on the other hand, couldn't stand Aunt Marsha even though she was his sister. He and Mum sometimes had arguments about it.

"Why don't you try being polite to your sister? Getting to know her?"

"I grew up with her! I know enough! I don't want to know any more!"

The funny thing was, whenever Aunt Marsha came to stay it was amazing how busy Mum suddenly found herself. "I'm so sorry, Marsha," she'd say, "I have to go and see a friend of mine today — she's sick and needs my help," or "I have to do some extra work at the shop — I'm afraid the kids will have to entertain you today. But I'll be back later. . . ." And then she wouldn't come back for hours and we'd be stuck with Aunt Marsha.

Once when Dad's oldest mate, Jack Tiges, came over and he and Dad were drinking beer together in the backyard, we heard Dad say that he couldn't stand his sister, Marsha. We heard him say that she was a bossy, nosy bully and that the best day of his life was the day he got into his rattletrap two-thousand-dollar VW (that sounds like a lot but it's really cheap for a car) and left Canberra so that he could live as far away from Marsha as possible.

And now they were telling us we had to make her feel welcome while they went on their winter trip *for three whole weeks*! Mum and Dad always took a vacation in the middle of winter, but it was only ever for four days to Coffs Harbour — never for three weeks to *Paris*.

Usually we got to stay with the Giannopouloses next door. Stella (that's Mrs. Giannopoulos) made souvlakia (that's meat on a stick) and spanokopitas (they're cheese and spinach pastry things but you can hardly taste the spinach) and every night we stayed we had ice cream with Ice Magic and Leo (Mr. Giannopoulos) played cards with us and once he showed us how to do Greek dancing and he said I was a *natural*.

There were so many of us, counting the Giannopoulos boys — they were Stella and Leo's grandkids and they lived next door to Stella and Leo — that we got away with anything, but Mum said that three weeks was too much for the Giannopouloses since they had five grandsons hanging round so much of the time, and it would have to be Aunt Marsha.

"It's not fair!" said Aidan. Aidan was only seven and he said *It's not fair!* about a hundred times a day. This time he was right.

"Yeah!" agreed Vince, who was nine and had learned that saying *It's not fair!* never changed anything. "You would never spend three whole weeks with Aunt Marsha. You'd rather eat worms!"

"That's true," said Dad softly.

"I heard that!" snapped Mum, flicking Dad with a tea towel. "Your father and I have never had a three-week vacation — we've saved up for a whole year for this, and we might as well tell you that we're going to Paris — *to get married!*"

"You're already married!" Vince and me said together.

"We know that," she said, "but we're going to get married again. It's called renewing your vows. It's to bring the romance back."

"Where did it go?" asked Aidan, pushing his glasses back up his nose and sticking a spoon into his boiled egg.

"Good question." Dad grinned before his face turned serious. "Listen, kids, your mum and I really need this, and your aunt really, well, she really — she isn't so, well, she's not *so* bad. . . ."

"Liar, liar, pants on fire!" sang Vince.

"Watch out, Dad, your nose is growing, just like Picchonio's!" said Aidan.

"It's *Pinocchio,* stupid!" I looked at Mum. Her back was to us while she did the dishes so I couldn't see her face. I knew what it would look like — tired. She'd be thinking, "I've got to do the dishes, I've got to get the kids off, I've got to get Dad organized, I've got to do this, I've got to do that. . . ."

I'm eleven — twelve in three months — and I understand about romance. Romance is about roses and the moon and long movie kisses. Parents love it. Mum and Dad bought a stock and feed shop last year, which is about as far away from roses, moons, and movie kisses as you could get. Mum spends all her time mixing birdseed, measuring out dog wormer, and rubbing her sore back. I guess Paris might be good for her.

COUNT-DOWN

I**T'S A COUNTDOWN NOW — TWENTY-NINE DAYS TILL MUM** and Dad go to Paris. Mum bought a little book with a red-white-and-blue cover called *Speak Easy French*. Now she says *Passez-moi les pommes de terre* instead of "Pass the potatoes" and *Voulez-vous de la crème anglaise?* instead of "Care for some custard?" Dad keeps grabbing her arm and kissing her all the way up and down it and saying, "Oh, ma chérie," like Gomez from the Addams family. Mum starts giggling worse than Tammy Nicks from our class who is always in trouble for in-class giggling fits. I think the romance is *already* coming back. It's disgusting.

AIDAN'S NIGHTMARE

THE NIGHT BEFORE AUNT MARSHA WAS DUE TO ARRIVE Aidan woke up crying from a nightmare. Dad heard him and came in and turned on the Scooby-Doo light beside Aidan's bed. When he asked him what the matter was Aidan just said, "Aunt Marsha, Aunt Marsha," and cried some more.

By now Vince was awake, too, and sitting up in his top bunk.

Dad had on the voice he used when one of us had a hard time at school, or hurt our knee falling on the gravel, or lost at cards more than three times in a row. "I'm sorry, kids," he said, helping Aidan put on his glasses. "I know your Aunt Marsha can be a bit tough on you, but you know how much Mum needs this vacation, and me, too, we both need it. We've been working so hard at the shop and —"

"But why can't you just go to Coffs Harbour for four days like you always do?" Vince asked him.

"Because, well . . . because your mum always wanted to get married in Paris and we couldn't afford to do it then, and now finally, after all these years, we can — *if* your Aunt Marsha comes and looks after you. It's very kind of her really. . . ."

"But what's Paris got that Coffs Harbour doesn't?" asked Vince, who's still too young to know about Paris art galleries and restaurants with white tablecloths and candles and French bread. Vince thinks Coffs Harbour is the best place in the world because of Sea World and the Giant Slide.

"Paris . . ." Dad shook his head, closed his eyes as if he was already in Paris in his head, and put on his French accent. "Ahh gay Paree, ooh la la, ze Eiffel Tower, oh ma chérie, ze croissants, ooh la la!" I felt like pushing him off the bed.

"But Dad," I interrupted, "Aunt Marsha . . ." I knew I was whining.

"I know, I know," he said, opening his eyes again. "But

when I come back, we'll get Jack over and have a cricket match and you can tell us every single horrible, bossy, nosy, annoying thing she does and I promise I won't get cross if you need to say a few rude things about her as long as you behave yourselves while she's here, OK, kids? Please say it's OK. We want to know you understand and that you'll try to be good while we're gone. Otherwise we'll be worried about you and we won't have a good time and your mum really needs a good time. She's been getting too tired lately, you all know that."

"Will you bring us something back from Paris?" Vince asked.

"Keep your voice down, Vinny, Aidan's already asleep," Dad whispered. "Of course we'll bring you something back. How about a nice, sweet-smelling cake of French soap for each of you?"

"Da — ad!" Vince and me whined and Vince hit Dad with the pillow.

"I'm kidding, I'm kidding!" Dad laughed. "Of course we'll bring you back a fantastic surprise, something special for each of you, OK? Now, get to sleep, you guys, it's very late."

■   ■   ■

I lay in bed and thought about Paris. Every different city is famous for things that everybody's heard of, even if they haven't actually seen them. Like Melbourne being famous for the Flinders Street steps and Canberra being famous for the man-made lake and Paris being famous for the Eiffel Tower. I've never seen the Eiffel Tower. "Eiffel" is a funny word. Eiffel, *Eiffel*. Maybe it's the French way of saying *Awful*. Maybe it's the *Awful Tower*.

A PHOTO OF AUNT MARSHA

TODAY WHEN I WAS IN THE LIVING ROOM I LOOKED AT THE photo on the mantelpiece of Aunt Marsha, Dad, and Uncle Nedley. They all look young in the photo — maybe they're even still at school. They're playing in the garden. Dad is laughing and hosing Aunt Marsha and Uncle Nedley, and they're trying to run away. Aunt Marsha is wearing a summer dress with sunflowers on it and her long wet hair is half hiding her face as she runs away. Uncle Nedley looks exactly the same, only smaller. He's wearing little shorts with a belt. A dog is in the picture, too. He is jumping through the water with his mouth wide open.

A YEAR AND A HALF AGO

I<small>T'S BEEN A WHOLE YEAR AND A HALF SINCE WE LAST</small> saw Aunt Marsha. Not last Christmas but the Christmas before, when her and Uncle Nedley had The Big Fight. The whole family was there: Aunt Fay and Uncle Bob, all our cousins, Nanna Jude, Uncle Nate and his de facto Rina who comes from Italy (a de facto is like a wife but there's no ring or wedding dress or anything), plus all the family extras like Jack Tiges and our neighbor Boris Rivik who can't speak much English and his dog, Growls, who growls but doesn't mean it.

We were all sitting around the table stuffing our faces with turkey and cranberry sauce and potatoes and peas when we began to notice there was an argument going on and it was coming from Aunt Marsha and Uncle Nedley's corner of the table.

"They're useless, Marsha, and it's time you admitted it." That was Uncle Nedley, and we all knew that he was talking about the Royal Family. We also knew that Aunt Marsha absolutely loved the Royal Family. She has a thing about them. Dad says maybe Aunt Marsha was a long-lost member, or she wanted to be. Uncle Nedley had a thing about the Royal Family, too, only his thing was an opposite thing to Aunt Marsha's. He couldn't *stand* the Royal Family and he made sure he always told Aunt Marsha just how much.

"Useless? Who are you to call anybody useless? You, who's never done an honest day's work in your life?" That was Aunt Marsha, speaking in her most British accent. Aunt Marsha spoke a bit like someone from the Royal Family, which made my theory of her actually being *from* the Royal Family so likely.

"Oh, you're so stuck-up, Marsha! That's why you like the Royal Family, because they appeal to your stuck-up snobbery!"

Nobody spoke to Aunt Marsha like that. Even Growls went quiet.

"The day you get off the dole and do an honest day's work, then I will be prepared to debate with you the current position of the Royal Family!"

I'm not sure what being "on the dole" is, but from Uncle Nedley's reaction I got the picture that it's maybe worse than being on drugs. Uncle Nedley's face went very red. "Sickness benefits," he hissed back at Aunt Marsha.

"Ha!" she said. "You don't fool me. I'm a nurse, remember? I do know about real sickness, and your knee got better years ago, Nedley."

I knew that Uncle Nedley had a sore knee, because he still had a limp, but whatever Aunt Marsha had said to him seemed about the worst thing you could ever say. Dad looked stunned. Mum's mouth dropped open. Only Boris kept eating.

Suddenly Uncle Nedley picked up Mum's white cranberry sauce dish, held it for a second with his hand shaking, and then just turned it upside down and smashed it on Aunt Marsha's plate, dumping cranberry sauce all over Aunt Marsha's turkey, potato, and peas. You could hear the plate smashing underneath the white cranberry sauce holder. After that everything went really quiet.

Then Aunt Marsha looked at Uncle Nedley with her eyes pinched up and said, "Manners, baby brother." She wiped her mouth with her napkin, pushed her chair back, got her handbag off the sofa, and walked out of the house.

Mum got up and chased after her but came back by herself. Aunt Marsha was gone. Uncle Nedley was crying and saying to Dad and Jack Tiges that his knee was still bad and that Aunt Marsha knew it. He said she'd always thought he was hopeless and tried to run his bloody life and he was sorry for ruining everybody's Christmas.

Suddenly Boris looked up and asked if he could have some of the cranberry sauce from off Aunt Marsha's plate. Everyone cracked up laughing, as if that was the funniest thing anyone could ever do. Boris stopped chewing for a minute and said, "Vot funny?" Everyone laughed even more.

Mum rang Aunt Marsha that night and said sorry on behalf of Uncle Nedley, but we haven't seen Aunt Marsha since. Till now — starting from tomorrow we're going to be living with her for *three whole weeks.*

A KNOCK AT THE DOOR

AUNT MARSHA IS DUE TO ARRIVE ANY MINUTE. SHE'S GOING to have dinner with the whole family tonight and then, tomorrow, we're all going to take Mum and Dad to the airport. There's a strange feeling in the house — it's like a part of Mum and Dad has already left for their vacation, as if they're only half here. They're pretending they're *all* here but we know that half of them is already in Paris — looking at Paris paintings in Paris art galleries, drinking Paris coffee, reading *Speak Easy French,* and getting their dumb romance back.

We were sitting round watching a dumb show on the telly

and Vince and me were pretending to laugh — pretending that we weren't just sitting there waiting for you-know-who to arrive, and Mum and Dad were pretending they weren't already half in Paris — when there was a knock at the door.

SHOE-BOATS

WHEN MUM OPENED THE DOOR AUNT MARSHA was standing there with a suitcase. She was bigger than how we remembered her. She was really big. She was tall with her hair in this big basket-shaped bun on her head. Her hands were big, and she had big fingers and a big neck and a big nose. Even her feet were big. I looked at them — I couldn't help myself. I knew it was rude and I should have been reaching up to kiss her cheek and saying, "Hello, Aunt Marsha," but I had a feeling her feet were going to be huge and I couldn't resist taking a look. And I was right! They *were* huge — they were like big shoe-boats at the end of her legs. And they stood out more because her shoes were white. Really bright white. I guess those shoes reminded her of her hospital days because they were like nurses' shoes.

I looked across at Aidan, and I could tell he was about to cry. His lip was jumping up and down and his cheeks were turning red. I shook my head at him and said in my mind *Pull yourself together, Ads, it's going to be OK. I'll look after you while Mum and Dad are gone, promise.*

See, a part of me did want to do the right thing. A part of me did want Mum and Dad to have a special time. Not all of me, but enough for me to want to do the right thing by Mum and Dad. And it worked. Aidan's cheeks went back to their normal color and his bottom lip calmed down.

WELCOME, AUNT MARSHA

MUM STEPPED FORWARD AND GAVE AUNT MARSHA A BIG hug. I don't think Aunt Marsha was so used to big hugs, because her arms just stayed stiff by her sides and her face had the same look on it as if someone had just stepped on her toe. "Wonderful to see you, Marsha. Thank you so much for coming," said Mum, taking her bags from her.

"Come in, Marsha," said Dad. His mouth was stretched into the shape of a smile but it looked like it was hurting his face. "Great to see you. You're looking terrific. Retirement must suit you." His voice sounded the same as when he had to talk to Mr. Meldine at a parent-teacher meeting. He seemed a bit scared of Aunt Marsha. I think we all were. "Say hello, kids!" Dad said, with the same strange smile. Aidan wouldn't let go of Mum. He hid his face in her hair and Vince and me knew it was up to us.

"Hello, Aunt Marsha," I said.

"Give your aunty a kiss, Tina," Mum said, pushing me forward. I reached up — it was a long way up there to Aunt Marsha's cheek. She was like an enormous tower. I reached up and Aunt Marsha leaned down and then I put my mouth on her cheek and I kissed. Her cheek sucked into my mouth a tiny bit but it was OK. The thing I noticed most was the smell. Cabbage. Cooked cabbage and rose perfume. Aunt Marsha loved cabbage, I remembered.

"Hello, Bettina," said Aunt Marsha. The sour cabbagey smell got worse when she spoke. And nobody calls me *Bettina*. Even Mrs. Stills at school calls me *Tine* or *Tina*. It's not that I don't like the name — it's an OK name for somebody else. Maybe someone called Bettina might wear their hair long over their shoulders, not in two ponytails like I do. They might be good at math and sewing, not like me. I don't like math or sewing. I like English and drama. A person called Bettina probably couldn't play soccer or have a best friend called Mish or be good at writing stories like me. I'm *Tine* or *Tina*, but not to Aunt Marsha.

Vince's turn. "Vince?" said Mum. "Don't be shy." Mum knows that Vince is never shy.

"Hello, Aunt Marsha," he said in an almost whisper.

"Hello, Vincent," said Aunt Marsha. Vince stood on tiptoes for his kiss. His eyes were closed — he looked as if he was swallowing cough medicine. Nobody calls Vince *Vincent* either. It's the name of Mum's favorite artist. She said when she was having Vince she kept seeing orange and yellow dots in front of her eyes. Those were this artist's, Vincent's, favorite colors. He used to paint a lot with them and so that's what she called Vince. But Vincent is more the name of someone who loves reading and cooking and long walks. Not someone who likes Nintendo and karate and telling dumb jokes. That's Vince, or Vinny.

"Aidan?" said Mum to the back of Aidan's head, since he was still hiding his face in her hair. "Are you going to give your Aunty M. a kiss?" I knew there was no way Aidan was going to do it. I was surprised Mum even tried. "He's a bit upset about us going — you know what they're like," she said to Aunt Marsha.

"I know what they're like when they're allowed to get away with murder," said Aunt Marsha.

"Well, come in, get warm, and have a cuppa. You must be freezing!" said Mum. Mum always suggested a cuppa at times when nobody seemed to know what to do next. I tried a cuppa once. The taste wasn't very nice, even after the three big spoons of sugar I put in mine when Mum wasn't looking. Anyway, adults love cuppas, especially my mum. She drinks them all day.

"Bah!" said Aunt Marsha. "Melbourne is positively warm compared to Canberra! I'm cooking under this coat!" I couldn't help imagining Aunt Marsha's whole enormous body cooking like a chicken in the oven underneath her big red coat.

CHOCOLATE BUTTON MUFFINS AND GALLSTONES

DAD TOOK AUNT MARSHA'S BAGS UPSTAIRS AND MUM WENT into the kitchen to make tea. "You kids look after your Aunt Marsha and I'll be back with the tea in a minute," she said.

Aunt Marsha went and sat in the Dad-only chair. Nobody ever *said* it was the Dad-only chair but only Dad ever sat in it. It was brown leather with an attached footrest that Dad liked to put his feet on when he slept in front of the telly sometimes. Aunt Marsha looked pretty comfortable in that chair. It was just about big enough for her. I wondered what Dad would think when he came downstairs and saw Aunt Marsha sitting in his chair.

Us kids sat in a row on the leaf-pattern couch. We never do that either. We just sit anywhere. On the floor usually. But now we were sitting on the couch in a row in our nice clothes with our hair all brushed and tidy like we were about to have our photo taken.

Nobody spoke. Aunt Marsha pulled her gloves off slowly, one finger at a time. They were proper white gloves like the Queen wears. Or maybe everyone in Canberra wears gloves like that, but I'd only ever seen them in movies from the olden days or on the Queen when she got in the news. Aunt Marsha patted her big basket-shaped bun. A few bits had come loose and she pulled them back into the basket shape. Then she took a lipstick from her purse with a little mirror holder, and drew on some more orange lips. She already had orange lipstick lips, so I wasn't sure why she did that.

At last Mum came back into the living room with the tea tray and some chocolate button muffins. Our mum makes the best chocolate button muffins ever. Usually she makes them for the Giannopouloses next door to say thanks for minding us kids.

"How have you been, Marsha?" Mum asked. "Rob was right — you do look well." Our mum's really good at making people feel happy but I don't know if it was working with Aunt Marsha. Her face had the same half-angry look.

"Hmm," said Aunt Marsha. "I haven't been too well, actually. I've had gallstones taken out, big as marbles the doctors said. All caught up in my bladder."

"Oh dear," said Mum.

"What are gallstones?" asked Vince.

"What's a bladder?" asked Aidan.

"How do you take your tea?" asked Mum.

"White and none, thanks, Sandra," answered Aunt Marsha. That's tea-talk for milk and no sugar. If you live with my mum you learn tea-talk pretty fast.

Vince asked his question again. "What are gallstones?" Mum acted like she hadn't heard him.

"Thank you so much for coming to stay, Marsha. You know how much Rob and I appreciate it. We feel very lucky we've got you. And the kids are really looking forward to spending some time with you again, aren't you, kids?" Mum looked at us in this way that if we didn't say *yes* she might cry.

"Oh yes, yes we are," I said.

"What are gal — ?" Vince tried again.

"Be quiet, Vince!" Mum said, really fast and quiet.

"Well, Sandra, it suits me, too," said Aunt Marsha, reaching for a muffin. (I noticed that she was going for the biggest one, the one with the most chocolate buttons on top, the one I had *my* eyes on.) "You know how much I love children. Especially after all those years in the children's ward at the Royal Canberra."

Aunt Marsha opened up her big orange lipstick lips and took the first bite from her muffin. She looked at us as she chewed and the look seemed to say, *Now, listen here, you lot, if you don't behave yourselves like all those little kids wrapped in plaster in their hospital beds at the Royal Canberra, I'm going to eat you up and swallow you just as I'm about to do with this first bite of your mother's biggest chocolate muffin, the one with by far the most chocolate buttons!*

I knew without looking that Aidan was about to cry. I squeezed his hand, which I was holding in mine, and I said to him in my mind, *Don't cry, Ads. I told you it's going to be fine — I'm going to look after you, they're not going for that long, and it'll be OK, promise!*

It worked. His bottom lip settled down and his cheeks went back to normal.

TELEPATHY

IF YOU REALLY WANT TO SAY SOMETHING TO SOMEBODY BUT you can't say it in words, because maybe it would sound rude to somebody else who might be standing there (like Aunt Marsha), or because the person you want to say something to is far away and can't hear you, then you can do what I just did with Aidan. You can think the words really hard in your mind and imagine them sailing through the air and going straight into the ear of the person you want to speak to.

It's called telepathy, and I think it only works with people you know well, like brothers or best friends. Sometimes it works with Aidan and sometimes it doesn't. I found out it was called telepathy because Hamish Clive, the naughtiest boy in class, said he could do telepathy on Mrs. Stills to make her not give him a detention. When Trace Aitken asked him what telepathy was, he told her and I told him I'd been doing it on my brothers for ages and that if he wasn't careful I'd use telepathy to make him ask Mrs. Stills to marry him.

YOUR AUNTY'S RIGHT

"**W**HY DON'T YOU KIDS GO OUTSIDE AND PLAY WHILE your Aunty Marsha and I have our tea?" Mum still sounded nervous.

"Sure, Mum. Come on, you guys," I said to the others, getting off the couch. Vince reached out for another muffin as he stood up.

"Surely one muffin will do, Vincent? You don't want to spoil your appetite now, do you?" Aunt Marsha said, holding Vince by the wrist.

Mum's face twisted up for a second, then she did this funny little laugh. "Your aunty's right," she said. "Now off you go and play." Vince dropped the muffin, pulled his wrist away, and ran out of the room. Me and Aidan followed him.

"They really aren't used to us going away for so long," we heard Mum say to Aunt Marsha as we were leaving. But I knew that wasn't why Vince ran out of the room like that.

SAD QUIET

THE LAST FAMILY DINNER AT 1 MACLUSKY STREET BEFORE Mum and Dad left for Paris was very quiet. Aidan didn't sing and Vince didn't crack any jokes or eat dessert. It was apple crumble with custard. Vince loves apple crumble with custard. I think the muffin incident scared him too much. Aunt Marsha's grip on his wrist looked pretty tight.

Aidan held up one of his Brussels sprouts on the end of his fork and asked Aunt Marsha if it was the same size as one of her gallstones. I'm not really sure what gallstones are but I think they're made of blood and they're bad for you. I knew Aidan shouldn't have asked about them anyway. Dad laughed when Aidan asked, but Mum said, "Don't be silly, Aidan."

Then she said, "Sorry, Marsha, he's not trying to be rude — he's just curious."

Aunt Marsha went, "Hmph," and kept on eating.

Dinners at our house are usually pretty noisy. It's the time when we get to tell each other everything that happened in the day. If any of us wanted to say what someone had said to them in class or at the shop, or tell how we fell over in the playground or say a knock-knock joke we'd heard, dinner was the time to do it. Sometimes it seemed everyone wanted to tell their bit at once and Dad had to say, "Come on, folks, one at a time!"

Usually there's one or two of the Giannopoulos kids eating with us, too. All of the Giannopoulos kids are noisy. They say they have to be because there are so many of them that if they didn't shout nobody would pass them anything at the table or laugh at any of their jokes.

Sometimes dinners might be quiet if it's something really special we're having — like fish and chips — when everyone's too busy eating to say much. But tonight wasn't one of those nights — tonight it was just chops and veggies — and it was very quiet.

Aunt Marsha didn't seem to need to talk. She just sat

there chewing on her chops. Maybe she didn't know how noisy dinners at 1 Maclusky Street usually were. If there was any talking Mum was doing it. She talked about how this winter was really a lot colder than the other winters, and about how cloudy it was all the time, and how there'd been not much rain, and how sometimes there'd be a bit of sun but not much, and how it was usually a bit windier at this time of year. I'd never heard Mum say so much about weather.

NOT WITHOUT ME

I DIDN'T SLEEP SO WELL ON THAT LAST NIGHT BEFORE MUM and Dad went away. I dreamed a lot and kept waking up. Some of the dreams I couldn't remember properly, only the feeling from the dream, but there was one dream I did remember. Vince and Aidan and I thought we could fly. We climbed up to the top of the roof of our house. We were going to jump off. When we got to the top Aunt Marsha was waiting there, holding on to the chimney. She took my hand and said, "Not without me," and then I woke up.

THE LAST TIME AUNT MARSHA CAME TO STAY

THE LAST TIME AUNT MARSHA CAME TO STAY SHE COOKED for the family and we had to eat it all because otherwise Mum said Aunt Marsha would be upset. Mum came outside to the swings where we were playing and said, "Now listen, kids, your Aunt Marsha is making a special dinner tonight. I'm not sure what she's making. It does smell a bit different than what you're used to, but I want you to be polite and eat it all up, OK?" By the way Mum said this we knew dinner was going to be really bad.

And it was. It was scary. I didn't want to ask but I think I ate a fish's eye. I felt it slip down my throat before I could cough it up, even though I had a good try. There was a lot of cabbage and cauliflower, too. The dessert had bran in it like Grandad eats. Vince said, "Hey Aunt Marsha, did you know Grandad's bran's in this?" and Dad kicked him under the table. Well, he meant to kick him but he kicked me instead, so I kicked Vince, like in Chinese Whispers where you pass it on. Vince said, "What?" in this loud voice even though he knew he shouldn't have asked Aunt Marsha about Grandad's bran.

THE LONGEST THREE WEEKS

IT WAS THE LAST FAMILY BREAKFAST AT 1 MACLUSKY STREET. Mum and Dad were rushing round still packing things, so they couldn't really sit down at the table and talk. Dad didn't have time to boil eggs, he burned the toast, and Mum left her tea to get cold. She never does that.

Dad said we should take our car to the airport because it's bigger and Mandy could come in the back, but Aunt Marsha said she wouldn't feel comfortable driving back home in it and dogs shouldn't even go in cars and that she'd rather take hers. Aunt Marsha's car is a lot tidier than ours. There are no empty orange juice bottles or chip packets on the floor and no dog hairs on the backseat like in ours. Aunt Marsha's car is tidy and small and the same color orange as her lipstick.

Aunt Marsha said there were only three seat belts in the backseat, so one of us kids would have to stay back with the Giannopouloses. Vince and me knew it was out of the two of us. I knew I'd have to be there to look after Aidan once Mum and Dad were gone in case he got upset. We all knew that next to Mum and Dad I handled Aidan the best.

"It's OK," said Vince, "I'll stay." You could tell he wasn't happy about it.

"Vinny, you're a hero," said Mum, giving him a hug. Vince's eyes went red.

"I'll take you across," Mum said, taking him by the hand. He let her, even though these days Vince doesn't let anyone hold his hand.

Seeing Vince's eyes going red like that made me feel like crying, too. It was silly. It was only three weeks. Three weeks was nothing. Three weeks was only as long as midterm break. Three weeks was only one week times three. It wasn't even a whole month! Mum and Dad would be back before September even got started. But it didn't matter what I told myself, the next three weeks suddenly seemed like the longest three weeks in the world. I felt the most upset about it when I saw Mum take Vince's hand and him not pull it away as they walked next door with Mandy to the Giannopouloses'.

When she came back, Mum looked upset herself. "He's OK," she said to Dad as they carried their suitcases to the front door. "Stella gave him some ice cream and let Mandy sit on the couch."

"He'll be fine," said Dad, rubbing Mum's shoulder. "Come on, Sandy, it'll be OK. We need this vacation." Dad looked at me. "You're OK about this, aren't you, Tine? You'll look after the boys and be good for your Aunt Marsha, won't you, sweetheart?"

A part of me wanted to stamp my feet and scream and say, "It's not fair!" like Aidan does, but I'm eleven — twelve in three months — and those day are over. I took a big breath and I said, "Sure, Dad."

AIRPORT DRIVE

AUNT MARSHA AND DAD GOT IN THE FRONT SEATS AND me and Mum got in the back with Aidan in the middle.

"Seat belts, everybody!" said Aunt Marsha as the car pulled out of the driveway. Aunt Marsha's head nearly touched the roof and her bum was pouring over the edges of her seat.

Mum asked Dad a couple of times if he had the tickets and did they pack the guidebook and what time would it be when they got to Paris, then everything went quiet again. The news on the car radio was the only bit of talking. A news lady was saying how a man loved rock climbing so much he tried to climb down from the top of the tallest building in Sydney. He got stuck halfway when his shorts got snagged on a ledge. The man had to be rescued with a helicopter and he was crying and saying, "I *really* love rock climbing." The news lady said he had to be treated for shock. I think if Vince was here he would have liked that story.

So far Dad and Aunt Marsha had been pretty nice to each other. Dad was making a real effort not to be rude or say, "Oh, give it a *rest*, Marsha," the way he usually did. But still, when you were in the same room as both of them, even if they weren't having an actual argument, you could *feel* an invisible current of argument between them all the time, as if they were only just managing not to fight. In some ways I think it would be easier if they just got it out of the way. I think they were about to do that now.

"Can't you go a bit faster, Marsha?" said Dad. "You're holding up the traffic."

"I'm going quite fast enough, thank you very much," Aunt Marsha said, sounding cross.

"Marsha, it's just as dangerous to drive too slowly as it is to drive too fast, you know."

"Shush, darling," said Mum. This was one of those times

when she'd say *How about a nice cuppa?* but she couldn't very well do that in the backseat of Aunt Marsha's car halfway down the airport freeway.

"I have never had an accident in my car, Rob. I don't think you can say the same thing, can you?" Aunt Marsha knew very well about Dad's accident when he wrecked the VW. He ran over a dog. The dog didn't die but he did lose a leg. Dad still feels bad about it.

"That was years ago, Marsha. I can't believe you would bring it up!"

"Your driving hasn't changed a bit though, has it?"

"The accident had nothing to do with my driving! The dog ran out in front of me!"

"Well, if you'd been driving more slowly that dog might still have four legs!"

"Marsha, that is total *crap!*" Dad was getting pretty angry.

"Settle down, love," said Mum from the backseat.

"Why should I settle down? I didn't start this!" said Dad.

"Well, you did actually, Robert. By criticizing my driving!"

"I did not criticize your driving!"

"You did!"

"Did not!

"Did!"

"DID NOT!"

They were worse than Vince and me when we got going. Suddenly Aidan burst into big, wet, noisy Aidan tears. I had to put my hands to my ears, he was so loud. I think he'd been holding on to those tears ever since Dad gave us the bad news all that time ago. Now he was making up for it, and he didn't have much time left, since we were nearly at the airport.

"Ads darling, it's OK. Aunt Marsha and Dad don't mean it, they're just having a bit of fun — aren't you, Rob? Marsha? You love each other, *don't you, Robert and Marsha?* You are brother and sister, after all!" Mum put her arm around Aidan and held his hand. He kept snuffling for a bit but soon everything went back to quiet. Except for the radio. It started to play "If You Leave Me Can I Come Too" with Aidan joining in and singing in a soft sniffly way *We can always stay* until Aunt Marsha turned it off.

Mostly, drives out to the airport are fun. It's always exciting to pick up Uncle Nedley coming all the way from Darwin — he always looks brown and happy to see us. He picks us up and throws us right over his shoulders and says, "You kids are bigger than Darwin camels!" Or picking up Rina and Uncle Nate from the airport when they came back from Italy. Rina's from Italy and she needs to go back a lot to see her mum and dad. I like watching all the people come back to their families. Sometimes they cry because they haven't seen each other for so long but mostly they just look really happy. This trip out to the airport was nothing like those others. This one was awful.

SAYING GOOD-BYE

"**G**OOD-BYE, MUM, GOOD-BYE, DAD," I SAID.

"Look after the boys, won't you, sweetheart?" Mum whispered in my ear.

"Yes, Mum," I said. "Have a great time." That last bit was the hardest to say. In some ways I wanted them to have a terrible time. I hoped it would be raining and I hoped all the restaurants ran out of French bread and I hoped all the hotels were already full and I hoped that the croissants were stale and I hoped that the stupid Eiffel Tower that Dad told me about had fallen down and that there was nothing left to see in stupid dumb Paris. But another part wanted it to be good for them, too. That other part did hope they got their stupid romance back, even if it made Dad act like Gomez and Mum giggle worse than Tammy Nicks. I just didn't know which part was in charge — the two parts seemed to be having a fight right in my throat so I couldn't talk properly.

"Love you, Tines," said Dad, as he let go of me.

I couldn't say *I love you* back. The fight going on in my throat was hurting too much. I hope Dad understood that I did love him but that I just couldn't say it right then.

"Come on then, enough's enough!" You can guess who said that. "Time to get back. Vincent will be waiting."

"Good-bye, darlings, we'll bring you something back! We love you!" And then they were gone as the double doors closed behind them.

For a minute, just a tiny minute, we stood there — Aunt Marsha, Aidan, and me — not quite knowing what to do. It's like we were in a shock — as if we were saying to ourselves, "What happens now?" It only lasted a tiny, tiny minute. Maybe it was only me who noticed it because I'm such a big noticer of things. The whole family knows it. If something's lost they say, "Just ask Tine, she'll know where it is!" because I'm a noticer. I notice where people leave things, I notice the way people say things, I notice what they wear, I notice moods, I notice if things change. And I noticed this tiny minute when we didn't quite know what to do next.

"Come on, children. Enough fussing about! Back to the car!" Like I said, the minute didn't last long. Aunt Marsha pushed us toward the doors and out of the airport.

"I'll ride in the back with Aidan, Aunt Marsha. I think he might feel better if I do that."

"Nonsense, girl. You must stop babying your little brother. He's quite old enough to ride in the back by himself — aren't you, Aidan?"

Aidan shook his head. He wanted me to sit with him in the back. "I don't mind sitting in the back, Aunty Marsha," I said.

"I know you don't *mind*, girl, but I mind. Aidan is not a baby and you will sit in the front seat and that's the end of it." Aunt Marsha's orange lipstick lips snapped shut and I got into the front seat beside her. Aidan got into the back. I turned to him and gave him a smile. It was my best cheer-up smile, but I could tell by Aidan's red cheeks that it didn't work.

BUGS EATING ROSES

EVERYTHING WAS QUIET IN THE CAR ON THE WAY HOME. At least Aunt Marsha turned the radio back on. Aidan sang softly along with the man on the radio *Hot legs it's a quarter to four, I love ya honey* until Aunt Marsha changed it from singing to talking. A man was talking about these tiny bug things that attack roses in the summer. He was saying how they bite little holes in the petals and then put poison onto the edges of the hole until the rose started to die slowly. Aunt Marsha looked the most excited that she had since she came to stay. She kept nodding and going *Hmm* and *Oohh* like the bugs eating the roses was the most exciting thing she'd ever heard.

I looked out the window and tried to count trees, but they were going past too fast. I noticed some birds flying over us in a big V-shape and then it started to rain and I wondered if the birds got wet would they get cold. I was going to ask Mum but then I remembered it wasn't Mum in the seat next to me, it was Aunt Marsha, so I just went back to wondering about the birds on my own.

A few times I turned round to check on Aidan. His cheeks were red but the bottom lip was staying still. He was staring out the window, too, but I don't think he was trying to count anything. His face looked blank. Sometimes it's hard to tell with Aidan, what he's looking at or what he's thinking, because he wears such thick glasses. He has to — he has bad eyes. He doesn't mind them too much except that when he first got them he was teased at school. Tracey Denham and Mike Hammer called him *Foureyes* and Aidan came home crying. I went and told them the next day if they called him that again I'd punch them. I've never punched anyone before (except Vince when he stole my Walkman) but I'd punch Tracey and Mike if they called Aidan *Foureyes* again. I didn't need to. They were nice to him after that.

MANDY'S GIFT

WHEN WE GOT BACK TO THE HOUSE MANDY CAME racing out to meet us with something in her mouth. Mandy liked to greet us with a present when we got back from places and she hadn't come.

"Whatever is that in the dog's mouth?" said Aunt Marsha as she got out of the car.

"It's a present for you, Aunt Marsha!" said me and Aidan laughing, as Mandy wagged her tail and ran round in circles.

Mandy dropped the present at Aunt Marsha's feet.

"Oh dear! Oh no! Oh my goodness!" Aunt Marsha wailed. I looked at the present that Mandy had dropped at Aunt Marsha's feet. A very large pair of creamy brown underpants lay in the mud. They weren't mine, and they weren't Mum's and I don't think they were a pair of Dad's either. They looked too big. Suddenly I knew who the knickers belonged to.

"That horrid dog!" screamed Aunt Marsha. "From now on, that dog stays *outside*!"

"But Aunt Marsha," I said while Aidan rushed to Mandy and put his hands over her long black ears so she couldn't hear, "Mandy didn't know they were your — your —" Suddenly I didn't know what to call them. "She probably thought they were Dad's old ones. She just wanted to give you a present!"

"I don't care!" said Aunt Marsha, picking the knickers up out of the mud. "A dog's place is not in the home! From now on Mandy must live *outside*!"

"But Mandy has always lived inside!" I said.

"Well, as long as I'm here she stays outside, and that's the end of it!" I wanted to suggest that as long as Aunt Marsha was here perhaps *she* could stay outside. I could tell Aunt Marsha meant what she said, the same way she meant it when she said we had to take *her* car to the airport, and the same way she said I had to sit in the front seat.

I knew there was going to be trouble with Vince over this. Even though Mandy was the family dog, in a way she was more Vince's than anyone else's. She slept on Vince's bed, he took her for the most walks, he patted her the most, he was the one who fed her snacks and gave her the most cuddles. I couldn't say what he was going to do when he heard she had to stay outside.

"Now you two go inside while I go and collect Vincent from the Gia — Gian — Gi —" Aunt Marsha was having trouble with the name. It was a tricky one at first, but once you got the hang of it, it was a great one to say. I loved saying it. *Giiaaannnooppouulooos.*

"Giannopoulos," said Aidan, helping her out.

"Hmph!" Aunt Marsha didn't seem too interested.

"We'll go and get Vince, Aunt Marsha," I said. I really felt like seeing Stella and Leo and maybe being the one to break the bad news to Vince. And I could see that Aidan really needed one of Stella's hugs. I thought Aunt Marsha would be happy about us going next door for a bit. Mum usually was. She said it gave her a chance to get some housework done. When we came back the house always looked the same as it did when we left. I think Mum just liked the peace and quiet. Aunt Marsha didn't seem to want us to go at all.

"No," she said. "You two go inside and I will collect Vincent. I want to meet Mr. and Mrs. Gia — Gia —"

"Giannopoulos," Aidan and me said together.

"Inside, you two! I will be back shortly."

PICASSO CALENDAR

AIDAN AND ME WENT INSIDE AND I PUT A RED TICK IN THE *August 1* box of my Picasso calendar. Picasso was an artist who painted things however he wanted to. If he felt like painting a lady with an ear growing out of her head and only one eye and green hair, then that's what he would do, and he got famous for it. I don't know many famous painters, but even if I did I think Picasso would be my favorite because he paints things how they look in my dreams. The picture on the August page is a bird carrying a leaf in its beak. I love this picture because it looks like the bird is carrying the leaf as some kind of present, maybe for another bird. I got the calendar for Christmas from Mum and so far I hadn't written anything on it. Except for one red tick. I was going to put a tick in every day that Mum and Dad were away — when there were twenty-one red ticks Mum and Dad would be back.

A DIFFERENT SATURDAY

USUALLY ON A SATURDAY MORNING WE'LL GO OVER TO the Giannopouloses' for a game of soccer in their huge backyard. It's more like a park than a backyard. It's got a hill in it and tall trees and a vegetable patch. Stella screams at us for trampling over the zucchini plants but that only happens when the ball goes out of play. I think Stella likes kids a lot and that's why she likes having all her grandsons over and doesn't mind our visits. She says she's glad her boys are with her and Leo while their parents are at work and not on the streets doing drugs or down at the mall getting girls pregnant. Nick is the oldest Giannopoulos kid and he's only thirteen. I think that's probably too young to be at the mall getting a girl pregnant, but Stella worries about that sort of thing. It's because she's from the older generation.

Sometimes I'll get Mish over to play, too. Mish is my best friend and one of the reasons is that she loves soccer, too. She's pretty good at it. Her only problem is that she's small and she gets knocked over a bit. She never seems to mind that much — she just bounces straight back up and yells, "*Penalty!*"

I knew not to invite Mish over this Saturday. I just had a feeling that Aunt Marsha would make a fuss about it, even though Mish is usually pretty polite (except maybe when she's playing soccer and someone does a handball).

The Giannopouloses usually have a couple of cousins over too, plus Uncle Pavlos. Uncle Pavlos's wife left him fifteen years ago for the mechanic, Stella told me, so he liked the company on the weekends. Sometimes there's a pretty big gang of us. We split up into two teams and set up goals made of stakes from the vegetable patch. Sometimes we play until it's almost dark and Leo calls out, "*Ella na fame, pethia!*" That's the Greek way of saying "Come inside and have some dinner." We stay for dinner, too. If we go to leave Stella grabs us and says, "*Oxi, prepi na kathisete.*" That means "No, you must stay and eat with us." Then she rings Mum to check that it's OK, which of course it is.

"What do you want to do, Aidan?" I asked as we looked around the empty house.

"Comics," he said. Aidan really loves comics. He's got the whole *Phantom* collection, all the *Spider-Man* and *Simpsons* comics, *Star Trek* comics, *Star Wars* comics, *Archie* and even some *Betty and Veronica*, which are the only ones I like. Whenever Aidan reads comics he moves his lips slowly and he doesn't hear if you say something to him. The other thing about Aidan is that he knows all the words to songs. He loves Classic Hits FM. Mum and Dad reckon he's gifted. Mum and Dad only ever know the first few words of a song. Mum might be making dinner and she'll just start a bit of singing — *Goodbye, Norma Jean* — and then Aidan, without even looking up from his comic, will finish with *I never knew you at all*. Mum just about falls over every time he does it. She can't believe he can remember all the words. That's why she reckons he's gifted. I suppose he is pretty clever in his own comics and singing way.

Aidan wandered upstairs to his room and I waited for Vince to come back. Soon I heard them coming through the front door. Vince ran straight up the hallway, up the stairs, and to his room. He didn't even look at me. Uh-oh. Mandy must have tried to come inside. I went upstairs and into the boys' room. Vince was lying on his bed with his face in the pillow.

"Hey Vince," I said. He didn't say anything. I sat on the edge of his bed. "Vince?" I said again. Still nothing. "Come on, Vince, Mandy loves being in the garden. Maybe we can put a hot water bottle in her kennel at nights. . . ."

"No!" said Vince, into the pillow. I could tell he was crying. He really loved Mandy. Vince used to wet the bed till Mum and Dad let Mandy sleep with him.

"Come on, Vince, it'll be OK. Maybe, maybe I could ask Aunt Marsha again. Maybe she was just mad 'cause her knickers got all muddy. . . ."

"I hate Aunt Marsha!" he said, all muffled and teary into the pillow, like a little storm. Even though I could so easily have said, "Me, too, I hate her even more," I knew that it was my job to say she was OK. That's the thing with being the oldest — there's certain jobs that you have to do just because you're the oldest.

"Aunt Marsha just doesn't know how much you love Mandy, that's all. Maybe in Canberra all the dogs live outside. . . ."

Vince wasn't talking. I didn't know what to say to him to make him feel better.

"How was the Giannopouloses'?" I tried. "Are they playing soccer?"

Nothing.

"Vince? Come on. Talk to me. Did you play soccer?"

Still nothing. I thought for a minute till I had a good idea.

"D'you wanna have a game with me?"

"What?" At last.

"D'you wanna have a game of soccer with me?"

"Where?"

"In the backyard."

"Not big enough."

"Yes, it is!" I said, even though I knew it was going to be a bit of a squash. Mum and Dad don't reckon our backyard's big enough even for a trampoline. They said if they put a trampoline in there'd be no room for barbecues or picnics and Mum said she was scared one of us would knock a tooth out so she wasn't too keen on the idea. Which was a bummer, because we really wanted a trampoline. The best thing about our garden was the tree house.

TREE HOUSE

UNCLE NEDLEY AND DAD BUILT IT TOGETHER WHEN IT WAS the Queen's Birthday. On the Queen's Birthday everyone has a holiday so that the weekend goes for three days instead of two. Uncle Nedley kept saying, "Well, the Queen does come in handy for some things," and then he'd laugh and keep hammering.

Our tree house wasn't square and neat and easy to climb up to, like the Aitkens' across the road. That's what made ours so great — it was a bent triangle shape with an upstairs. It had shelves and a sink in it and it was pretty tough climbing to get to. You had to learn how to bend your body around the branches and you had to know where the missing rungs in the ladder were. When you were at the very top of the ladder you had to reach out for the branch on the left, the one with the butterfly chimes (Mish and I hung them there for music), put your feet on the branch on the right, and pull yourself up into the tree house. It's probably lucky that Mum's never been up because I don't know if she'd be too happy about that last bit where the ladder finishes.

When it was really windy the tree house moved. It was like being on a boat on a stormy sea. We pretended to be pirates and put Aidan upstairs in the crow's nest (that's not a real crow's nest that a real crow lives in — it's this little wooden lookout thing high up on a pirate ship. Pirates sit in it and look out to sea and when they can see an island coming they shout *Land Ahoy!*).

Our tree house was high up, too. Really high. Higher than anyone else's tree house I'd ever seen. That was because of Uncle Nedley. He kept saying to Dad, "Oh, come on, Rob, the thing has to be exciting for these kids — let's go higher!"

Aidan, who was the best climber in the family (mostly because he wasn't one bit scared of heights), liked to hang out in the tree house with Chris Giannopoulos. The two of them swapped comics and said, "What's the special password?" if you tried to come up. It was pretty annoying because if you didn't know the password, which nobody ever did, they might say, "Begone, enemy!" and throw orange peels at you.

Vince went up there by himself when he got in big trouble with Mum and Dad. He sulked until it was dinnertime and Mum had called out about a hundred times, "Vinny, come down, dinner's ready!" He always did come down, but not until Mum said, "*If you don't come down now I'll send your father up!*" We all knew there was no way Dad would climb up and get Vinny but that was the sign Mum was at the end of her tether.

Me and Mish liked to go up to the tree house to talk in private and giggle our heads off without getting in trouble.

Vince and me and Uncle Nedley had even made a kind of harness out of Dad's old hay pulley so that we could get Mandy up and down the tree house. Mum and Dad used to sell hay bales at the shop to the kids in Baywood who were lucky enough to have their own ponies. The pulley was used to get the hay bales off the truck so that Dad didn't hurt his back. You pulled one end of the rope and Mandy went slowly up through the branches to whoever was waiting in the tree house at the top ready to pull her inside. The rope had a safety catch like rock climbers use when they're climbing down really high cliffs in case they fall. If the person at the bottom let go of the rope Mandy wouldn't go crashing down to the ground. The rope would catch and Mandy would hang there in midair waiting for us to pull on the rope again.

Mandy's a Labrador, and Labradors can get pretty big. Mandy's huge, probably because of all the toast crusts and apple cores and chop bones that Vince feeds her, so the rope harness had to be big and strong. Uncle Nedley helped us get it onto the tree. Mandy liked being up in the tree house and she never made a fuss when Vince tied her into the harness. We called it "The Mandy Lift." Mum wouldn't let us use it anymore because she thought it was dangerous and got cross with Dad and Dad said it was all Uncle Nedley's idea.

THE GAME AND NOT GARDENING

"THERE'S NOT ENOUGH PLAYERS WITH JUST YOU AND ME," said Vince.

"We'll get Mandy to play, too! And Aidan. Come on, Vinny, it won't be a proper game like at the Giannopouloses', but it'll still be a game. Come on." I grabbed his hand and pulled him up off the bed.

"Race you downstairs!" Suddenly Vince was back and charging down the stairs.

"Ads!" I yelled out to Aidan, who was reading comics on the living room floor.

"Where are you going, young lady?" Aunt Marsha stepped out of the kitchen with an apron round her waist.

"We're — we're just —" I didn't know what to say. I was sure that Aunt Marsha wouldn't let us play soccer. She'd think of a reason why we shouldn't — probably that it was a bit wet and gray outside and we'd all have to go inside for the day. "We're going — we're just —" I was still stuck.

"We're going to do some gardening!" said Vince. "We always do on Saturdays, don't we, Tine?"

"Yes, every Saturday," I agreed.

"Gardening . . . hmmm." I didn't know if it would work. "Well, Sandy and Rob are teaching you something useful then, aren't they? Off you go then. Stay warm. I'm baking fig biscuits for later. It is always important to weed I suppose. . . ." Aunt Marsha went back into the kitchen and Aidan, me, and Vince raced outside.

Vince got the ball from the shed and I set up some goals down the side of the house — that way Aunt Marsha couldn't see us not gardening and playing soccer. It was Mandy and me against Vince and Aidan. I don't think we expected to have as much fun as we did. We played like we were at the Giannopouloses' and it was the real thing. When we ran, we really ran, when we kicked we really kicked hard. It's like we were so angry at that ball, we wanted to kick it all the way to Canberra. Sometimes Mandy ran off with it, which stopped the game and made us laugh, but it was only a minute before we got it back from between her teeth and got going again. Whenever the ball got kicked anywhere near the back window where Aunt Marsha might be able to see us, Vince went and got it back carrying the shovel high over his head in case Aunt Marsha looked out the kitchen window, which made me and Aidan laugh our heads off.

"Children!" We heard Aunt Marsha calling from the kitchen, sounding just like the Queen again. "Fig biscuits!"

By the time we had to go inside we were hot and thirsty and wet from the rain which we didn't even notice had fallen. That's soccer for you.

WHERE'S VINCE?

THAT NIGHT, WHEN I WENT IN TO SAY GOOD NIGHT TO Vince and Aidan, Vince wasn't in his bed. There was only Aidan in the bottom bunk reading *Archie's Weird Mysteries*.

"Aidan," I said, "where's Vince?" Aidan didn't answer me. He just kept reading his comic. "Aidan! Where's Vince?" Still he didn't answer me. I pulled the comic out of his hands. "If you don't tell me where he is I'm going to tear it in half!"

"Nooo!" Aidan whined.

"Well, where is he?"

"I can't say."

"What do you mean you can't say? Why can't you say?"

"Because I made a promise."

"What promise?"

"A blood brother promise."

"Aidan, I'm in charge of you now that Mum and Dad are away and you have to tell me where Vince is!" I couldn't help feeling worried.

"Well, I can tell you that he's outside," Aidan said.

"Outside? What's he doing outside?"

"I can't say."

"You can say, Aidan."

"But we did a blood brother promise. If I tell then one of us might die." He looked really scared.

"OK then, Aidan. Well, I'll just have to go outside and look for him myself, won't I?"

"I think so. . . . Sorry, Tine . . ."

I tiptoed past Mum and Dad's room, where Aunt Marsha was sleeping, and went downstairs and out the back door into the garden. It was a pretty cold night. What would I tell Mum and Dad if something happened to him? The garden was full of noises. I had to tell myself it was just the wind and the possums and not the ghost with long white fingers like I've been scared of since I was small.

"Vince!" I called out. "Vince!" No answer. I walked down

to the shed at the bottom of the garden and opened the squeaky metal door. "Vince? Are you in there?" I climbed over the old couch and three hay bales, past the boxes of bottles and newspaper and Dad's fishing gear. "Vince? Vince, come out if you're in here!"

Mandy came up behind me and licked my hand. "Mandy!" Suddenly I knew where Vince was. I ran out of the shed to Mandy's blue wooden kennel, the one Grandad built. "Vince?" I said as I bent down and peered inside.

"What?" answered a grumpy-sounding Vince. He was curled up in a sleeping bag.

"What are you doing out here?"

"I'm sleeping with Mandy."

"You can't! You'll freeze!"

"Will not. This sleeping bag is Dad's thermal one. I took it from his closet. I'm staying out here."

"Vince, come on, this is silly."

"Well, go inside then."

"Vince, please come back inside. I'll ask about Mandy again tomorrow."

"I already tried. She said no. I'm sleeping out here until Mum and Dad get back and let Mandy inside again." Vince sounded as sure as Aunt Marsha when she wouldn't let Mandy come inside. I thought maybe I should go and get Aidan and the two of us could stay with him, but the kennel looked full as it was. I wasn't sure what to do. I couldn't tell Aunt Marsha. She'd go crazy. I suppose it would be OK if Vince stayed warm enough. And I could come and get him before anyone else woke up in the morning.

"Well, I'll go and bring you a hot water bottle and another blanket, OK?"

"OK. Can you bring me a pillow, too?"

I went back into the house and got the things from upstairs. Luckily Aunt Marsha stayed in her room. I don't know what I would have said to her if she had come out.

After I brought Vince out his sleeping things I set the alarm for six o'clock so that I could go and get him in the morning. Then I went into Aidan's room and sat on the edge of his bed.

"Did you find him?" Aidan asked me.

"Yeah, I found him," I answered. "Hey, Ads," I asked him after a bit, "do you think it's OK if I let Vinny stay out there with Mandy?" I know Aidan was only seven but he was the only person I could ask. I wasn't exactly going to ask Aunt Marsha.

Aidan was quiet for a minute, and then he said, "Did he get Dad's thermal sleeping bag? The one he bought in case he ever went camping in the snow?"

"Yeah," I answered.

"Then I reckon it's OK. Mandy loves Vince a lot."

"Yeah, I know."

"Maybe you should stay in here in Vinny's bed. . . ." I think Aidan didn't want to be alone. And I didn't really either.

"Good idea, Aidan," I answered.

CARTOON MORNING

I GOT VINCE UP AT SIX O'CLOCK AND HE CAME BACK TO BED. He said he slept like a log. He got that one from Dad.

"Vince, next time you can take the alarm clock and get yourself up — I can't do this every morning," I told him. I was feeling tired and annoyed. "And if you don't, you'll get busted by Aunt Marsha and she'll make you sleep inside, OK?"

"Sure, Bossy," said Vince, crawling back into his own bed. Sometimes Vince made me want to pinch him. But not this morning. He looked pretty tired. I wondered how logs actually did sleep. Did they have feelings, did they dream, did they snore and roll around in their log beds?

See, that's me, I wonder about a lot of funny things. I can sit around for hours just wondering about things. Mrs. Stills calls it daydreaming and gets cranky when I do it. She doesn't know I'm wondering about important things in my head and maybe working out some answers to some pretty important international questions — like if logs sleep, and if a blanket of snow keeps you warm, and what time it is in Paris right now.

Sunday mornings are always cartoon mornings. Mum and Dad sleep in and we stay in our pajamas and turn the heater on. We go and get the corn flakes and the rice puffs and bowls and milk and sugar and eat our way through the lot in front of all the cartoons and *Dancerama*. Vince and I are too old for *Dancerama*, but Aidan likes the songs and he's in love with Cathleen, one of the girls in the show, so sometimes we put up with it. We join in the dancing (just to make Aidan happy). Mum and Dad know we're breaking the no-telly-in-the-mornings rule but they don't mind because it's Sunday. It's like we've woken up before the house has and we're having fun in a sleeping house. Nobody is saying yes or no to us and we can have as much sugar on our rice puffs as we want.

We were carrying our bowls into the living room when

Aunt Marsha came in wearing a lime-green-and-black track-suit. Her face was red like she'd been for a jog, even though her hair was still in the big basket shape on her head. You would think that would make jogging pretty hard. Keeping all the hairs in place — you'd have to use a special sort of glue, a special sort of extra-strong hairspray glue. . . .

"Goodness me, children! Sunday morning and the television on! Just because the parents are away doesn't mean the mice can play!" said Aunt Marsha in a singsong voice. She was smiling. Jogging must have put her in a good mood.

"We always watch telly on a Sunday morning. It's when Mum and Dad sleep in," said Aidan. It was time for *Dancerama* soon and I think he was scared he was going to miss Cathleen.

"Well, that's just plain sneaky then, isn't it, Aidan? Watching it behind their backs?"

Aidan was quiet. He didn't mean to say they were sneaky. He wanted to say it was OK to watch it on a Sunday morning but somehow he hadn't put it right.

"What Aidan means —" I tried to explain.

"Let's not fuss about what Aidan means, Bettina! Television off this instant!"

"But Aunt Marsha —" I tried again. Mostly because of

Aidan. I was reading *The Lion, the Witch and the Wardrobe* and Vince would probably be happy to play Nintendo but Aidan really liked that Cathleen and the cartoons. Maybe watching the cartoons was like watching all his comics come to life.

"Enough! Television off!"

Aidan got up slowly and quietly and turned off the television. This worried me more than if he'd started bawling his head off the way I expected him to. Next he walked out of the room and upstairs. Slowly, without a word. Aunt Marsha watched him. She seemed surprised, too.

"Well, he knows it's easier to just do as he's told," she said after a second. "Now, children, I want you to put on some outdoor clothes. And get your little brother — we're going to play some games in the garden. The children at the hospital used to really enjoy them. And they're wonderful exercise, too."

I looked at Vince. For a tiny second I thought we might both laugh, and if things weren't so awful maybe we would have.

"Come on, Vince," I said. "Let's get changed." Vince stayed sitting where he was. For a minute I thought he wasn't going to move at all. I looked at him and I said the longest *pleeaaase* in my mind that I could. Vince got up and headed upstairs.

OUTDOOR GAMES WITH THE BARONESS

"CATCH, BETTINA!" AUNT MARSHA THREW ME A RED rubber ball that she must have brought down from Canberra especially. She reminded me of the Baroness from *The Sound of Music* (my favorite movie) — the bit when Maria goes back to the abbey and the Baroness tries to be friends with all the kids and makes them stand in a circle and throws a ball to them and they all look really bored and sad because they miss Maria so much. Except that Aunt Marsha was a lot bigger than the Baroness and the Baroness was pretty.

I caught the ball and threw it really hard and high over Vince's head. "Catch, Vince!" I yelled.

"Bettina, don't throw the ball so hard! Vince couldn't possibly catch that!" said Aunt Marsha.

"Catch, Aidan!" Vince threw the ball super-hard at Aidan. It hit him in the face. It's funny, because Vince wouldn't normally do that. We all know to be a bit careful with Aidan because he's smaller than us and he wears glasses and can't see so well. Aidan started crying. I ran over and checked his nose and eyes. He was OK. The ball knocked his glasses off but they weren't broken. Still, he was pretty upset.

"Get back, Bettina! Let me see him!" boomed Aunt Marsha, rushing over. Aidan really started crying then. "Go on, stand back, Bettina, let me see his face. His nose could be broken!"

"It's not broken, Aunt Marsha. He's OK. He just got a fright, he —" I tried to tell her.

"Bettina, I was a nurse for over forty years! Now *stand back!*"

Aidan only liked a few people and a few different things. He liked his comics and singing, he liked Chris Giannopoulos who was born on exactly the same day as him, he liked Cathleen from *Dancerama*, he liked the tree house and the radio, and he liked Vince and me and Mum and Dad. A lot of other people and things he didn't like at all. That was just Aidan. You couldn't make him be different. I'd seen Mum try sometimes and it never worked. She tried to make him be friends with more kids at school. She'd invite them over and Aidan would ignore them. She'd try to make him read other things besides comics and he didn't like that either. Aidan drew pictures on books.

"Show me your face, Aidan. Your nose could be broken!" Aidan tried to pull away from Aunt Marsha. "Aidan, keep still!" Aunt Marsha held him in a pretty tight-looking grip. I guess she'd had a lot of practice doing that at the hospital when the kids didn't want to take their medicine or get a needle in their bums.

"He's all right, Aunt Marsha — really." That was Vince. He knew as well as I did that Aunt Marsha was only going to make things worse with Aidan.

"I can take care of this!" she snapped as Aidan wriggled in her arms. He was howling now. Next Aidan did something I'd never seen him do before. It would be easy to say that it happened by accident, and that's what I would say to Aunt Marsha. But what Aidan did next wasn't an accident. He kicked Aunt Marsha as hard as he could, on her leg just under her knee. It took Aunt Marsha by surprise, you could tell. Aidan must have been a better kicker than the kids at the hospital — some of them must have had sore legs so they had to lie still — but Aidan gave her a really hard one. You could tell by the way Aunt Marsha screamed and let go of him. Mandy started squealing and licking everyone behind the knees.

Aidan rushed inside as soon as Aunt Marsha let him go. I wanted to run after him but I didn't think it was the right thing to do. I had to make sure Aunt Marsha was OK.

"Is your leg hurt, Aunt Marsha? Are you all right?"

"That child kicked me! Little monster!"

RIGHT AND WRONG

WHEN I WAS VERY SMALL I DIDN'T THINK ABOUT right and wrong very much. I just did what I wanted and Mum or Dad told me if it was right or wrong. When I got bigger I learned for myself what was right and what was wrong. Right was setting the table, tidying my room, being quiet in class, and not teasing Vince. Wrong was leaving banana peels under my bed, giggling with Mish in class, running up and down the supermarket aisles and knocking over the soup cans, and teasing Vince.

Now that I'm eleven there are some things I know are right, some things I know are wrong, and some things I'm not sure about. For those things I might ask Mum or Dad.

"Mum, do I have to invite Trace Aitken to my party when she won't share her markers with me at school?"

"Dad, should I tell Mrs. Stills that I saw Tim Henshaw stealing chalk so he could write a bad word on the footpath?"

I think now was one of those times, too. Should I run inside and look after Aidan, or should I stay outside and be nice to Aunt Marsha? And Mum and Dad weren't around to ask.

What's hard about these times is that there's usually something you'd really *like* to do, like scream back at Aunt Marsha, "*You're* a monster!" and kick her just as hard on her other leg, but at the same time you know there's something you really *should* do. Like let Aidan look after himself this time and make sure that Aunt Marsha wasn't hurt.

"Are you OK, Aunt Marsha? Aidan didn't mean to hurt you. . . ."

Aunt Marsha was rubbing her leg. When she looked up at me she looked sad. I wasn't expecting that. I know why Aidan kicked her. All the same I wished he hadn't. I felt confused. I looked across at Vince. He was just standing there. He didn't look any more certain of anything than I did. But I was the one who was eleven. I was the one who had to know what to do next.

"Vince, go inside and talk to Aidan," I said. "Aunt Marsha, do you need a Band-Aid for your leg?"

"No, no really — I'm fine." Her nose sounded a bit sniffy and her eyes were red. "Go inside and make sure your brother's all right."

CAN STELLA HELP?

AIDAN WAS READING *STAR TREK ADVENTURES* ON THE FLOOR of his room with the radio playing *I should be so lucky — lucky lucky lucky*. Kylie Minogue. He loved her as much as Cathleen from *Dancerama*.

"Is your nose all right?" I asked him. He nodded a *yes*. "Aidan, you shouldn't have kicked Aunt Marsha like that."

"I didn't mean it," he said, not looking up.

"Yes, you did."

"No, I didn't."

"Well, just don't ever do it again." I said, leaving him to *Star Trek* and Kylie.

I went downstairs and got a drink from the fridge. While

I poured the orange juice into my glass I wondered about the orange juice in Paris, if they had it and if it tasted the same and if they didn't have it what did the kids drink in the mornings or any other time they felt like something cold and orange and sweet but stingy at the same time. Aunt Marsha was sitting in the Dad-only chair reading a book. She smelled like disinfectant and lavender mixed.

"I hope your leg is all right, Aunt Marsha," I said.

"It's fine, Bettina. And Bettina, please finish your drink in the kitchen, otherwise you're sure to spill it everywhere. Your mother might be happy to spend her life cleaning up after you, but I am not."

"Yes, Aunt Marsha," I said as politely as I could. I felt like throwing the rest of my orange juice on the carpet. Suddenly I had an idea. "Aunt Marsha, usually on a Sunday I go over to the Giannopouloses' to help Stella with Josie's babies. Josie works at the shop on Sundays and Stella really needs the help." It wasn't exactly true. I mean Stella did look after the kids and Josie did work at the shop on Sundays but I'd never helped with the babies before. I mean I said hello to them and maybe played with their toes for a second before going outside for soccer but I never really *helped*. If

Stella did ever ask me to help I wouldn't mind, so in that way it was true. I really wanted to see Stella.

"Hmmm . . . Your mother didn't mention anything about helping Stella on Sundays. . . ."

"Oh, she always likes me to go and help," I said. Vince wandered into the room. "I was just telling Aunt Marsha how we usually go and help *Stella* with the *babies* on a Sunday."

"What?" he asked.

"The *babies*," I said, making my eyes go wide and trying to do telepathy on him.

"Oh yes, yes, *the babies*," he said as if he knew exactly what I was talking about. Vince could be good that way.

"Well, I suppose it is a neighborly thing to do. And it will give me a chance to get the kitchen sorted out. It's a real mess in there. Off you go then. Be back by two, please, children."

We raced next door. Stella was drinking coffee — she drinks about as many coffees as my Mum drinks teas. She was talking on the phone in Greek. The only word we understood was Yiannis. Yiannis is the Greek way of saying John. That's Stella's son and the boys' dad. Yiannis is usually in trouble with Stella for something, so she always sounds cross when she speaks to him on the phone. Yiannis is always kissing Stella on the head and saying, "Don't nag, Mum."

Chris and Nick came into the room and they started doing karate kicks and pretend-boxing with Vince.

"Out! Outside! Get out of my kitchen!" Stella said, as she put down the phone.

"Go on, guys," I said, "go and play." I really wanted to have a private chat with Stella.

"Yeah yeah, we're goin', we're goin', don't get ya knickers in a knot!" Nick gave me a pretend karate kick and grabbed an apple before heading outside with Vince and Chris.

Stella came and gave me two cheek kisses (they always do that in Greece). "Ah Tina, you must be very sad without your mamma and baba, but lucky you have your *thia* to look after you." (*Thia* is the Greek way of saying "aunt.")

"Stella —" I began. I didn't know what I wanted to say or how I expected Stella would be able to help. One of those fights was going on in my throat again. Stella gave me another hug. Stella always smelled like honey and coffee mixed. I stuck some baklava in my mouth (baklava is cake made with lots of papery pastry with honey in between) and whatever was fighting in my throat had to take a break to deal with it.

"Hey *kooklaki moo*, child, wassa matter? You missing your mamma and baba, I know, I know." Stella has a lot of funny names for us. I think they mean things like "angel" and "chicken" and other nice things. She always grabs our cheeks and kisses us when she says them.

"Aunt Marsha —" was all I could manage to get out.

"Tina, Tina." Stella sat me down at a kitchen chair. "*Thia* Marsha is not your mamma, I know, but she love you, she has come a long way to look after you. Have you ever drive in the car to Canberra? Long way, *matakia moo*. You must be good for her."

"But, but . . ." I didn't know what I could say without sounding spoiled and horrible. "Mandy has to stay outside!" was all I could come up with.

"Ah! At last! All dog should live outside. In Greece we never have dog inside — smelly hairy *pah*!" Stella waved a hand past her nose and smiled. "Tina, your mamma come and see me before she go. She say please to make things easy for *Thia* Marshy."

Hearing her say the name wrong suddenly made me want to laugh.

"See, you feeling better! I think it is my baklava!"

I tried again. "But she won't let us come and play soccer. . . ." I felt like I was whining.

"It not for long, Tina, *tria* week only. It good to take a break from soccer, good for my zucchini plants, too! Soon Mamma and Baba come back and soccer soccer soccer every day. Tina, your aunty have no children — is special for her to have you. Be good for her. You the oldest, the boys do what you say. You be good big sister while your parents away. They need good holiday. When they call on the telephone you say you having good time, OK?"

This wasn't turning out the way I'd hoped. But what did I hope could've happened? What could Stella do?

"Stella, do you need help with the babies?"

"What you talking about? Why? You think I don't do good job with my babies? What are you saying?" Stella shook her head. She'd never heard me ask anything like that before. We heard shouts and laughing coming from the garden. "You go and play outside now, Tina. They need you to boss them around." She smiled and I went outside. I didn't feel any better about the way things were, though.

Stella sent us home for lunch. Cabbage soup. At least I think that's what it was.

THE SMELL
BY SUNDAY

BY SUNDAY AFTERNOON EVEN THE SMELL OF THE HOUSE had changed. Usually our house smells breezy, because Mum leaves all the doors and windows open — or sometimes it might smell of smoke a bit from the nighttime fire, but now it smelled like something different. It was a hidden sort of smell — one you couldn't quite put your finger on. In fact you wouldn't want to put your finger on it if you did know where it was because it would probably be sticky and strange, or green and furry the way yogurt goes after it's been left in the back of the fridge too long.

Cabbage! That's what it was, cabbage. Aunt Marsha kept all the windows and doors shut tight and cooked cabbage.

She had a *condition,* she said, that only cabbage could fix. It's hard to imagine a condition that cabbage could actually *fix.* And the way Aunt Marsha cooked it, it was like eating compost. Vince said he'd rather eat compost but he didn't say it to her face. He knew there'd be trouble. But it wasn't only cabbage — it was Aunt Marsha's perfume, too, and the way it *mixed* with the cabbage that made the smell of the house so different.

COLD, DARK BROWN, AND TIDY

AT FIVE O'CLOCK AUNT MARSHA CALLED US INTO THE DINING room for dinner. Even though we have a dining room, normally our family eats in the kitchen. The dining room is Mum's special room and it never changes. The Vincent pictures of sunflowers that she hung on the wall ages ago, the three green glass vases, the Chinese fan, and the statue of the lady carrying a bowl of water have all stayed exactly where they were. Everything else in the house seems to change around or get lost and make space for new things. But not in the dining room. Mum says it's for when guests come, and it's the only room that's not allowed to get messy. That's easy, because nobody ever feels like going in there. Even the guests — like Mum's best friend, Linda, or Rina or Uncle Nedley — they say, "Oh please, Sandy, let's just eat in the kitchen, not that dining room, it's too formal!" I think "formal" has something to do with cold and dark brown and tidy.

The dining room is Aunt Marsha's favorite room and it's where we now have to eat dinners. Aunt Marsha set the table with her place at the head and me way down the other end and Vince and Aidan on either side.

"Children," she said before we sat down, "have you washed your hands? Show me!" We held out our hands for Aunt Marsha to look at. We generally forgot to wash our hands before dinner and Mum and Dad generally forgot to make us.

"Disgraceful!" she said, turning our hands over. "Do you have any idea of the diseases you could catch? Amebic dysentery! Salmonella! Campylobacter! All killers! Now up you go and scrub those palms and fingers!"

So back up the stairs we went and washed our hands. "Can you smell dinner?" Vince asked me with his hands under the tap.

"Vomit," said Aidan.

"Shut up, Aidan," I said, although I could smell something pretty strange, too.

KIDNEY PIE

"**K**IDNEY PIE!" SAID AUNT MARSHA AS SHE PUT A BIG SLICE
of the black-colored pie onto my plate. I remembered Aunt Marsha's Kidney Pie from last time. Uncle
Nedley called it "punishment." He said, "Marsha, this is
pure punishment. Let's get takeout." Aunt Marsha looked
really upset. Mum said, "Nedley, your jokes are terrible.
Marsha, it's delicious!" but I noticed Mum hardly ate any of
hers. It's because kidneys are an *organ,* Dad told me, and
organs have a weird taste because they have jobs in the
body like taking away the *waste.*

Nobody spoke much at dinner. You could hear every
noise the knives and forks made when they scraped on the

plates. Aidan spilled his glass of milk and for a minute looked as if he was going to cry. Aunt Marsha looked at him and said, "Baby days are over, Aidan — nobody's interested." Aidan's bottom lip stopped jumping up and down and his cheeks went back to normal. Nobody can ever make Aidan stop crying if he doesn't want to. It made me feel mad. I wanted to stand up at the table and say, "If my little brother wants to cry then he can, it's his *right,* have you ever heard of *rights?*" But the truth was, just like Aidan and Vince, I was scared of Aunt Marsha.

Kidney Pie turned out to be Aunt Marsha's other favorite dish besides cabbage, and Vince said afterward that it tasted like cooked spew. I thought about explaining to him about kidneys being an organ for taking away the *waste* but it might have made things worse.

NOT DICKENS

AFTER DINNER, AUNT MARSHA ASKED US IF WE'D LIKE HER to read us a story. I've been reading on my own for ages now, Aidan has his comics, and Vince just doesn't like books.

"Ah, I think we'll just read on our own, Aunt Marsha," I said.

"Well, I think it's time Aidan put away his comics and tried something new. Aidan, you're getting too old for that rubbish now, aren't you?"

"It's not rubbish," Aidan said.

"Well, it's not Dickens!" Aunt Marsha laughed.

Vince laughed and said loud enough for only me to hear, "You mean Dorkens," and went upstairs. Vince likes Nintendo and PlayStation.

"Well, suit yourselves then." Aunt Marsha looked a bit sad. She must really like Dickens.

Aidan and me followed Vince upstairs. "I wonder if Mum and Dad are in Paris yet?" Vince asked.

"Shut up, Vince," I said. I seemed to be saying that a lot lately.

"You shut up," said Vince and went into his room.

After I'd been reading in bed for a while I heard Aunt Marsha coming upstairs. "Lights out!" she said, peering round the door.

"But it's only seven o'clock, Aunt Mar —"

"Lots of sleep means healthy bones, Bettina!" Aunt Marsha smiled at me before flicking off my light. She'd flicked it off so fast it took my eyes a bit to adjust — I kept seeing Aunt Marsha's smiling face still there in the dark.

After I'd been lying in bed for a while I heard Vince go quietly past my door. It looked like another night in the kennel. A couple of minutes later I went in to check on Aidan. He was asleep but I climbed into Vince's bunk just in case he woke in the night and got scared. At least I knew Vince would be warm enough. He'd kept the extra blankets and pillow hidden in the kennel with Mandy.

WAITING FOR MONDAY MORNING

NEVER BEFORE HAD US WENDLE KIDS LOOKED FORWARD so much to Monday morning and school. I wanted Monday morning to come more than I wanted to turn twelve. Even Mrs. Stills, my teacher, who I usually have a pretty rocky relationship with, seemed like Glinda, the Good Witch of the North.

I woke up early. Usually on Monday mornings I'll stay in bed and half-asleep till Dad comes in and says, "Tine — get out of there!" and throws a slipper or a sweater or something else off the floor at the bed.

For a minute I wondered where I was. The ceiling in my room has cracks in the shape of an arrow. The cracks in this ceiling were in the shape of lightning. It all came back to me in a hurry, like a big river of bad news rushing over me. Mum and Dad were in Paris looking for their romance and Aunt Marsha was here looking after us. Vince was in the kennel with Mandy and I was in his bed so Aidan didn't get scared in the night.

I heard Aidan roll over in the bunk underneath me and I knew I had to stay cheerful for when he woke up — that's part of the big sister job. The thing about the big sister job is you've got it for life. I would never not be the big sister. Even if I went and lived in the jungle in Africa to study the hippos (one of my dreams), I would still be Vince and Aidan's big sister.

The six o'clock alarm rang. I was going to have to get Vince up and out of the kennel again.

"Vince!" I whispered loud as I could at the two dark lumps in the kennel. No answer. Vince was a heavy sleeper. Mum said if a train went though his room he'd sleep right through it.

My bare feet froze on the wet grass. "Vince!" I said, hopping from foot to foot. "Wake up! It's six o'clock! Wake up!"

"What?" he groaned.

Mandy came out and licked my nose. "Don't, Mandy!" Even though it was Monday morning and I'd been waiting all weekend for Monday morning, I felt cranky. "Get up, Vince! It's six o'clock. Get up before Aunt Marsha finds out you're not in bed!"

"Aunt Mud Head you mean," I heard him say from inside the kennel.

"Just get up, Vince!" I didn't laugh, but I wanted to. *Aunt Mud Head.* That was a good one, but I couldn't tell Vince or he'd say it all the time till one of us called her that by accident.

Vince stuffed the blankets and sleeping bag in the back of the kennel and crawled out. "See ya, Mandy!" he said, giving her a hug.

We tiptoed past Aunt Marsha's room and back to our beds. There was no way I was going back to sleep and it was too early to get dressed for school. I picked up my book, *The Lion, the Witch and the Wardrobe,* and decided to read in bed for a while. What I like about books is you can get out of your own world for a bit and visit another one. That's handy if your world has an Aunt Mud Head — I mean an Aunt *Marsha* in it, and a mother and father in Paris. I was just up to the bit where Edmund is stuffing his face with all the Turkish delight the Queen of Narnia is giving to him as a trick. It got me thinking about how delicious Stella's Turkish delight was, how it stuck to your teeth and made your mouth turn pink. . . .

"Children!" Aunt Marsha's voice echoed through the house.

"Children! Up time!" Aunt Marsha opened my door. She was in another one of her tracksuits — orange and red this time — and she looked like she'd been jogging again. It hurt my eyes to look at it. "Up you get, Bettina. You don't want to be late for school!" There was no way that was going to happen. I wasn't going to miss one tiny second of school. I'd be seeing Mish and Laurie and Simon. I was even looking forward to hearing dumb Tammy Nicks's annoying giggle and seeing Mrs. Stills doing boring sums on the blackboard.

"Thank you, Aunt Marsha," I said. I won the politeness award when I was in Grade Five last year. Maybe I should've won the great acting award instead.

I got dressed and went into the boys' room to see how Aidan was doing. Sometimes Mum or Dad helped him, so I guessed it was up to me. If Aunt Marsha tried there'd be trouble for sure. She was probably too scared to come near him now anyway. He'd probably left a big bruise on her leg. Aidan was trying to put his shoes on the wrong feet but other than that he'd got everything right. I followed the boys into the kitchen. I was nervous as anything. We knew what Aunt Marsha's favorite drink at breakfast was. We'd had it when we visited her in Canberra.

GRAPEFRUIT JUICE

GRAPEFRUIT JUICE SQUEEZED FROM REAL GRAPEFRUITS. She said it "aids digestion." It must take something strong to break up all the cabbage and kidney pie.

There's only ever been one grapefruit in our house before. Mum decided to go on a diet and she started the diet with a grapefruit on the first morning. She stuck her spoon in the grapefruit and dug around in it for ages till she got a bit onto her spoon, then stuck it in her mouth. We watched her face squeeze up tight like a little raisin and Dad and me nearly fell off our chairs from laughing and then Aidan started to cry because he said Mum looked scary and Mum said,

"That's enough, everybody," and ate toast with apricot jam instead.

When we got downstairs there were three tall glasses of greenish-yellow grapefruit juice waiting for us on the kitchen table. Aunt Marsha must've brought the grapefruits down from Canberra with her. At least I could smell normal old toast cooking in the toaster.

"I'll go shopping while you're at school today," Aunt Marsha said, "but I'm afraid it's just toast this morning."

"I love toast," said Aidan, flicking on the radio. "It's my favorite," he said, before singing along to *Don't go changing to try and please me*. . . . It's true. Aidan loved toast and peanut butter. He'd live on it if Mum and Dad let him.

"No vitamins in toast," snapped Aunt Marsha. "Now drink your juice!"

The three of us looked at our glasses of juice like we were sizing each other up — the Wendle Kids verses the Grapefruit Juices. I went first. I tipped the glass upward and took a big sip. Aunt Marsha was watching me as well as the boys. I had to be a good example.

It was sour all right. I could feel my face doing what Mum's did that day. I think it's your mouth's way of trying to make the sourness go away. Vince laughed. *Your turn, Vince. Good luck.* Aunt Marsha turned to take the toast out of the toaster and quick as anything Vince put a huge spoonful of sugar in his glass and stirred. When she turned back he took a big sip from his glass. "Mmm, this is delicious, Aunt Marsha," he said and grinned at me.

"I'm glad you like it, Vince. It's pure — no sugar — and very good for you."

She turned back to the toast and I put a big spoonful of sugar into Aidan's glass and stirred.

"Drink up, Aidan," I said when Aunt Marsha turned back around. She watched as Aidan took a big drink from his glass. "Yum," he said, wiping his mouth.

"Good children," she said, looking pleased.

Wendle Kids 1, Grapefruit Juices 0.

We were about to leave the house for the walk to the bus stop when Aunt Marsha stopped us at the front door. "Uniform check," she said. She looked us over carefully, tidying our hair, straightening our collars, pulling bits of fluff off our sweaters. Mum would've loved this — she said she was worried we were the scruffiest kids in school.

She looked at Vince's shoes. "Scuffed!" she said to him. "Up you go and *shine,* Vincent." Vince just looked at her.

"That means your shoes need a polish, Vince," I said to him. I don't think he'd ever shined his shoes before. He'd probably been told to a few times but that didn't mean he ever actually did, and Mum and Dad didn't have the time to make sure he did. They had to be at the shop by eight o'clock for the dog food deliveries.

"Go on, Vincent, upstairs and shine those shoes! You don't want to miss the bus, do you? I suppose we could always do your lessons at home. . . ."

The thought of staying home all day with Aunt Marsha was terrifying. "I'll help him, Aunt Marsha," I said.

"Bah! Vincent is perfectly capable of shining his own shoes, aren't you, Vincent?" Vince still looked as if we were speaking in a different language.

"Go on, Vince," I said, "the polish and brush are under the bathroom sink. Quickly!" Vince looked at me, shook his head, and walked slowly upstairs. Aidan and me waited. Nobody said a word. Luckily our shoes passed the test, probably because Mum had bought us new ones only a little while ago.

At last Vince came back downstairs. We all looked at his shoes. I'd never seen them so shiny.

"New shoes," said Aidan.

"Not new, just shined." Aunt Marsha was smiling at us. It didn't make me like her any more, that smile.

"Come on, guys!" I said. "We'll be late!"

"Yes, off you go, children. I shall see you at three forty-five."

"Ah, Aunt Marsha," I said, "I sometimes go over to my friend Mish's house after school. . . ."

"Well, not today, dear. I have other things in store." There was no time to argue now and besides, Aunt Marsha had that *absolutely no way* sound to her voice.

The three of us walked down the street to the bus stop.

The sun was shining, Mrs. Aitken was hosing her roses, Jay Haley was crossing the street with his big sister, Margy, the postman was leaning over on his bike to put mail into Boris Rivik's mailbox — just like every other Monday morning. For a minute everything felt normal, as though Mum and Dad weren't in Paris but on their way to the Dinnings' to deliver twenty kilos of Pal for their three Dobermans.

Aidan stopped and turned back to look at the house. "She's still standing in the doorway waving."

"What?" Vince and me asked together.

"Look, turn round. She's still there." Aidan waved slowly. Like he didn't quite know what else to do.

"Oh God, I don't want to look."

"I wanna give her the finger." Vince grinned.

"Don't, Vince!" I said. Luckily just then the bus pulled up. *Mish!*

SCHOOL
AND MISH

"TEEEEEENNNNN!" SHE SCREAMED. FOR A SMALL PERSON she was very loud. Nobody on the bus even looked at her though — they were used to Mish's morning "Teeeennnn" scream. She was getting me into the habit. "Miiiiissshhhhh!" I screamed back. I think I was even louder than Mish this morning. She had this humongous smile on her face and she'd saved a seat for me.

"Hey Tine," she said, "how come you didn't ring me for soccer on the weekend?"

I groaned. "Aunt Marsha," I said, shaking my head. I didn't need to explain much more. That's the thing with Mish —

she understands a lot of things without needing them explained.

"How bad?" she asked.

"Very," I said.

"Maybe I could get my brother to kidnap you so you have to come and live at my house. . . ."

"What about Vince and Aidan?" I laughed.

"No way!" Mish laughed, too.

We didn't talk about the situation much more. I didn't want to.

TOAD FACE

I LAUGHED A LOT THAT DAY. WE GOT IN TROUBLE WITH Mrs. Stills even more than usual. "You girls are being unfair to everybody!" she said to us after class. I know it was naughty, giggling in class and whispering, but I couldn't help myself. It was Mish's toad face. Even when I just think about it I start laughing. I'm the only one she'll do it for because she says it's too ugly for anyone else to see. She squashes her face up with her hands and scrunches up her nose and tells that joke about the frog that goes to the library and says *Rread it, Rread it* every time the chicken tries to give him a book.

BEAN-AND-CORN-FLAKE PIE

"YOU WANNA COME OVER?" MISH ASKED ME ON THE BUS on the way home.

"I can't."

"Aunt Marsha?"

"Aunt Marsha," I said, as the bus pulled up to our stop.

"Three weeks isn't *that* long, Tine. . . ." Mish smiled in this hopeful sort of way and we waved at each other until the bus turned out of Maclusky Street.

"Welcome home, children!" Aunt Marsha had her apron on again. "How was school?" she asked as we came inside.

"Good, thank you, Aunt Marsha."

"Come and have some afternoon tea. I've been shopping and baking again today!"

Vince pinched me on the leg. Aunt Marsha pulled out chairs at the kitchen table.

Usually when we come home from school we'll slam our bags down on the table and one of us will go for the fridge and two of us for the cupboard. We'll pull everything out and yell, "Mum, there's nothing to *eat!*" at the same time as stuffing apples and chocolate biscuits and carrots and cheese and milk with cocoa into our mouths. Mum and Dad just stay out of the way.

Three glasses of water were already on the table. At least it wasn't grapefruit juice.

"Bean-and-Corn-Flake Pie!" Aunt Marsha beamed as she put the yellowish-looking pie on the table. It had brown bits in it — they must have been the beans.

"I made this one up!" said Aunt Marsha.

"Looks delicious, Aunt Marsha!" I said and took a bite. Lucky there was water at the table. You could tell Vince wanted to laugh watching me trying to eat that pie. He probably would've, except that he knew his turn was next. Vince actually did pretty well on this one. He loved cornflakes and he loved baked beans on toast, so I guess *thinking* that maybe made it easier to get the pie down.

"Can I have some toast, please?" Aidan asked. Everything went quiet.

"You had toast for breakfast, Aidan. Variety in the diet is important."

I was really tempted to ask Aunt Marsha, *Then how come you eat so much cabbage?*

"I like toast," said Aidan, looking down into the pages of *Spider-Man and the Aliens.*

"Well, perhaps you can have toast in the morning with your breakfast but you are not having it now. It's Bean-and-Corn-Flake Pie or nothing, I'm afraid."

"*Nothing!*" Aidan picked up his comic and ran up the stairs.

I was getting off my chair to go after him when Aunt Marsha stopped me. "Bettina, *leave* the boy alone! It's not good to indulge that kind of behavior! Now sit down and eat your pie!" I looked at Aunt Marsha. I wanted to take that plate of pie and throw it at the wall or, even worse, straight at Aunt Marsha. Suddenly I understood why Uncle Nedley did what he did with the cranberry sauce dish all that time ago. And if the phone hadn't rung just then maybe I would've done the same thing.

"I'll get it!" Vince and me said together, knocking back our chairs to get to the phone. For some reason, answering the phone just then suddenly seemed like the most important thing in the world. It was one of those wall phones and guess who was standing the closest to it?

A TELEPHONE CALL FROM PARIS

"**M**ARSHA WENDLE SPEAKING . . . OH, HELLO, ROBERT."
Mum and Dad!

"Aidan!" I screamed up the stairs. "Aidan! It's Mum and Dad on the phone! Quick!" Aidan came racing back down.

"Oh, that's nice . . . Oh yes, no it's all going well, yes they're well. . . . Yes . . ." Aunt Marsha was smiling into the phone while Vince did tiny little jumps up and down on the spot in front of her. "Well, they're very excited to speak with you so I'll put Vincent on. . . . All right then, well, goodbye . . . No, no need to call again, just enjoy yourselves!"

Aidan and me stood as close as we could to Vince to hear

Mum and Dad. Aunt Marsha watched as Vince spoke into the phone.

"Yes . . . Yes, um, no everything's — everything's OK, Dad, um." Vince looked back at Aunt Marsha as he spoke. "Yes . . . no, school was OK today. I kicked a goal, yeah! . . . And Mr. Denman said I might get best and fairest . . . Yeah . . . Well, I'll put Tine on. OK, love you, too, Dad."

I grabbed the phone.

"Hello, my darling!" It was Mum. The line was a bit crackly but she still sounded like Mum, even all the way from Paris. I could feel the fight starting up in my throat again. I could hardly speak. If I did I'd start crying for sure and I couldn't do that. Not with Aunt Marsha and the boys standing there watching me and listening to every word.

"How is everything, sweetheart? We miss you!"

"Yes . . . um, everything's OK. . . ." I wanted to say *I miss you too* but I couldn't. It's like there was already so much *missing* inside me that if I told Mum, my missing would take over and I'd have to join Mum and Dad in Paris and I'm not sure they'd be able to find their lost romance if I did that. I was eleven — twelve in three months — I had to set an example.

"How's . . . How's Paris?" I managed to squeeze out past the lump in my throat.

"What, darling?"

"I said *'How's Paris?'*"

"Yes, oh wonderful. Well, we only just arrived really. We're still a bit tired, but the hotel is wonderful. . . . Are you sure you kids are OK?"

I took a big breath. "Yes, Mum, we're fine."

"How's Aunt Marsha? Are you kids behaving yourselves for her?"

"Yes, we're being good for Aunt Marsha!" I gave Aunt Marsha one of my politeness award smiles. She looked relieved and smiled back. "I'll put Aidan on — he's going a bit mental."

In some ways it made it harder to speak when they were so far away. It reminded you of how much you wanted them to come back. Instead of making them feel closer, it made them feel even farther away.

"Hi, Mum. When are you coming back? Is that soon? Yes,

Mrs. P. gave me a star and I told everyone in news that you were in Paris and that you might eat a snail and that Dad might bring one back and I could show the class. Did you find the romance yet? Yes . . . What? We have to eat Bean-and-Corn-Flake Pi —"

I shook my head at Aidan and he didn't say anything more about the Bean-and-Corn-Flake Pie.

"Yes, I love you, too, Mum. . . . Is that soon?" Aidan started to cry then.

"Yes . . ." He cried into the phone. "When, Mum? Why not soon? I love you, too. . . ." He sniffed a bit and calmed down. Dad must've told him he was bringing him back the Eiffel Tower as a present. "Have you found the snail yet? The one you're bringing back? Yes, bye, Dad. Yes . . . Bye, Dad . . . Bye."

Aunt Marsha held her hand out for the phone. "That's enough, Aidan. Let me speak to your parents. Quickly now, it's very expensive. . . ."

Aidan gave Aunt Marsha the phone. "Yes, Sandra. No, they're being good, really good. Yes, oh I've been doing some reorganizing, yes . . . Look really, there's no need to call. . . .

Yes . . . Well, we'll speak to you next week then. Have a good time and we'll see you when you get back. Bye, Sandra."

"Well," said Aunt Marsha, hanging up the phone, "it sounds like they're enjoying themselves."

"They're missing us," said Aidan, before turning to go back up the stairs.

EXPENSIVE MONSTER

I WISH WE COULD'VE TALKED TO MUM AND DAD FOR LONGER. I wish we could've kept talking to them all the way through dinner and right up to when we got into bed and fell asleep — but I know it's too expensive. When Uncle Nedley comes to stay he sometimes rings up his girlfriend in Darwin and Dad says, "Come on, Nedley, get off the phone — it's too expensive!" And Paris is even farther away than Darwin.

Sometimes it feels like an Expensive Monster lives at 1 Maclusky Street. He hides behind furniture and under beds and it's like he's always hanging round waiting to spoil things. Whenever Mum and Dad start to talk about things being *expensive*, Mum chews on her thumbnail with scared eyes and Dad scrunches up his forehead and looks very hard at nothing at all and you would think that the Expensive Monster could leap out any minute and tear the house into pieces.

AUNT MARSHA'S ONE GREAT FEAR

AUNT MARSHA MADE US GET CHANGED AND DO our homework straightaway. She said that procrastination led directly to failure and that we needed to establish good work habits early in our careers. Vince looked at her as if she was speaking in another language again, and Aidan asked what a *career* was. Aunt Marsha told us that a career was a long and busy work path and that she'd chosen one over having a family.

"Do you have to choose?" Vince asked.

Aunt Marsha went a bit red and said no, she supposed you didn't.

So instead of playing in the tree house or getting under

Dad's feet at the shop, or snacking on Stella's food next door, or cuddling Mandy on the living room floor, we were sitting at the kitchen table doing homework. (I don't think Aidan had any homework but he was pretending he did because he always wants to be like Vince and me. He just drew airplanes in an empty exercise book.) Vince was behaving pretty well under the circumstances. He can be a lot wilder than this for Mum and Dad. I wondered if maybe he was being good for me, that if it was just him and Aunt Marsha it'd be a different story.

After homework and room-tidying and dinner and helping Aunt Marsha in the kitchen, we were allowed to watch the telly. Aunt Marsha said one of her favorite programs was on — *Getaway*. It's that show about little vacations you could take if you were married and didn't mind things being expensive. Mum loved it, too — she'd say, "Ooooh, doesn't that look lovely, Rob? But soooo expensive!" when they showed some tropical island vacation resort.

I wondered who Aunt Marsha would go on a *Getaway* holiday with since she wasn't married and her brothers didn't like her very much. Maybe she had some friends left over from when she worked at the hospital. Maybe some of the sick kids who'd gotten better had nice parents who really liked Aunt Marsha because she'd helped their kids to get better. . . . Maybe they wouldn't mind if she came along with them on a *Getaway* vacation. . . . Aunt Marsha said we could watch the show with her if we liked, and it had been so long since we'd watched telly we gave it a go.

Aunt Marsha sat in the Dad-only chair and we sat around on the floor. "Are you children comfortable?" Aunt Marsha asked us. I don't think she was used to people sitting around on the floor — but I love floor-sitting. You can really stretch out and put your legs and arms anywhere — over your head if that's where they feel like going.

"We're fine, Aunt Marsha," I answered. The lady on the show was explaining all about this daredevil vacation where you got to do all these scary things like bungee jumping and skydiving and stuff. Vince was loving it, but not Aunt Marsha.

"*Oooohh no, oooh my goodness, no!*" She hid her eyes behind her hands and went all squirmy in the chair while this man on the telly bungee jumped off a cliff. "*Ooooh that looks awful, ooohhh turn it off, turn it off, Vincent, pleeeease!*" She peered round from behind her hands as a lady on the telly skydived over another tall cliff. *"Oooh I can't stand it! Oh how dreadful — I feel sick!"*

"What's the matter, Aunt Marsha?" Vince asked.

"Heights!" Aunt Marsha looked white. "My one great fear is *heights!*"

REMEMBERING

THE THING ABOUT NOTICERS IS, THEY'RE REMEMBERERS, too. I remember everything. I remembered what Mum promised us if we were quiet in the supermarket, I remembered what Mrs. Stills taught us about the hippo's eating habits, and I remembered about Aunt Marsha's One Great Fear.

It was Easter. I was nine and Aunt Marsha was staying with us. Dad and Aunt Marsha took us on a bushwalk. Dad said, "Marsha, it's no problem if you just want to stay at home," and Aunt Marsha said, "You know how much I love the outdoors, Robert, of course I'm coming!" Even Aidan came. He sat in a special backpack for kids on Dad's back.

The bushwalk turned out to be a much longer one than Dad planned. After we'd been walking for ages Dad stopped under a tree to look at the map and give us all a drink from the water bottle.

"You never were any good at reading maps, Robert," Aunt Marsha said.

"That's not true!" Dad sounded annoyed.

"It is true — you're hopeless with them," said Aunt Marsha.

"If I'm so bad at them, then how come I was a head scout?"

"That was a long time ago, Robert, and don't you remember you got the whole group lost at camp?"

"That wasn't my fault! That was Sam Benty's fault. He dropped the map in the creek!"

"When will you take responsibility for your shortcomings, Robert?" Aunt Marsha said, taking the map out of Dad's hands. I didn't know what shortcomings were, but from the look on Dad's face they didn't sound like something you'd want to take responsibility for.

Aunt Marsha took over the map reading and said, "This way," when the track forked into two paths. I remember her singing *Hey ho, Hey ho, it's off to work we go* as she walked, and Aidan joined in on the *Hey ho's*.

We walked for ages along this track through the bush till we got to a special lookout place. That's where we found out about Aunt Marsha's One Great Fear.

Vince and me ran ahead and out onto the wooden platform to look at the view. I'd never seen so much forest stretching out in front of me from so high up. It made my chest feel like it was filling up with air. For a moment I was looking at the whole world. Vince said, "Wow, Tine, we're flying. . . ." as we held on to the rails of the fence and looked over.

Suddenly we heard Aunt Marsha screaming behind us. "No! No! Children, get back! Get back! Oh, Robert, get the children back from the —"

"Take it easy, Marsha. They won't fall, there's a fence there. . . ." Dad didn't sound worried at all.

"No, Robert! Get them back!" Vince and me didn't move. We'd never seen Aunt Marsha like that. We were shocked.

"Relax, Marsha, they're fine."

"Oh for goodness' sake, Robert, get them back! *Get them back!*"

"Marsha, you're scaring the birds. Relax, will you?"

Suddenly Aunt Marsha was running toward us. I think she

was going to try to pull us back from the edge. The next thing she tripped and fell over on the wooden platform. I remember the whole platform shaking as Aunt Marsha went flying forward on her stomach until her head was hanging over the edge under the bottom rail of the fence. She really screamed then.

"*Noooooo!*" It was the loudest, scaredest scream I'd ever heard — it rang out all over the bush, over the edge of the lookout and up into the sky. The whole world filled up with Aunt Marsha's scream.

Dad raced over to help her up. She was shaking and her face was white. I thought she might cry. After that we walked home and Aunt Marsha didn't say a single word for the rest of the day, not even in the car on the way back to 1 Maclusky Street.

That night, after Aunt Marsha had gone to bed with a nice cup of tea from Mum, I asked Dad why Aunt Marsha was so scared of being up high.

"It all started a long time ago, Tine, when your Aunt Marsha was little, maybe about Aidan's age."

"What happened?"

"Oh, something happened that gave her a fright."

"But what happened?"

"You ask a lot of questions, Tina. If I tell you I don't want you to tell your brothers. I'll tell them myself when they're a bit older."

"OK, Dad," I said. Sometimes when you're a bit older you get to hear important things first. "What happened?"

"Our big cousin Lenny came over to play. Lenny was mean — he had sticking-up red hair, I remember. He was tall and strong-looking and he was mean, always playing nasty tricks on other kids. Lenny played a very mean trick on Marsha. He told us kids to come and play with him at the bottom of the garden where there was a very high wall that separated our house from the neighbors'. We were scared of Lenny and always did what he told us, so we followed him. He told Marsha that if she climbed up the wall — he'd help her — he'd teach her to fly."

"Did she climb the wall?"

"Yep. Lenny pulled her up."

"Then what did he do?" I asked.

"He took her by the arms and dangled her over the wall. It was awful. It was a really high wall, and he dangled her over the other side. She screamed and screamed but nobody heard. He hung her over the wall and said, 'Marsha loves to fly, don't you, Marsha?' Then he shook her, the way you might shake the sand from a towel." Dad shuddered. "It was horrible."

"But what did you do? Did you go and get a grown-up?"

"No, no, we didn't. We were too scared of Lenny."

"What did you do?"

"We just stood there and watched. We were too little to know what to do." Dad shook his head.

"Then what happened?"

"Then he lowered her down and dropped her the last meter or so. That was the first time I really heard my sister scream a bit like she did today at the lookout. He dropped her into a bush. She was covered in prickles and she was shaking like a leaf, but she was OK."

"But did Lenny get into trouble?" I asked.

"Oh, Lenny was *always* in trouble. He's still in trouble. He had to move to America he got into so much trouble."

"I hate Lenny, Dad," I said after a bit.

"Well, Lenny has a few problems, Tine."

"And was Aunt Marsha always scared after that?" I asked.

"Of heights?"

I nodded.

"Yep. After that she didn't even like climbing stairs. We had to live in a house without an upstairs. Your Uncle Nedley and I were really annoyed with her for that. Yep. Heights are the one thing that sends your Aunt Marsha completely crazy."

"Heights and you and Uncle Nedley," I said.

Dad smiled. "Heights, me, Uncle Nedley, and smelly kids. That's four things. Now, go jump in the bath." He said it with a smile, but I could tell he was still thinking about mean Lenny and how he and Uncle Nedley just stood there feeling scared and watching and maybe waiting to see if Aunt Marsha could fly.

BUBBLING WELLS

FTER DINNER IT WAS READING TIME AGAIN, ONLY this time Aunt Marsha didn't ask us if we wanted her to read us a story. Instead she sat in the Dad-only chair reading her own book. It was called *Dickens: A Study of the Man Behind the Words*. She put another book on the little table beside the Dad-only chair. Maybe she had a strong feeling that *Dickens: A Study of the Man Behind the Words* could get boring and she wanted another book ready just in case. The other book was called *Magic of the Bubbling Well*, with *Mastering Tai Chi* written underneath. I wanted to ask Aunt Marsha how you could tell if a well was bubbling when wells were so deep in the ground, but Aunt Marsha had her reading face on and her reading face was sort of cross. She'd probably just say, "Bubbling wells are not for you, Bettina!"

It was early to bed again. That was after another fight between Aidan and Aunt Marsha about his comics. Aunt Marsha said they were not going to *take* him anywhere. Aidan said he didn't want to go anywhere, he just wanted to read his comics. Aunt Marsha said that reading is about *growth,* and Aidan said, "Spider-Man is better than *you!*" and raced upstairs.

Mish rang. I answered the phone and this voice said, "RRRreead it, rread it!" I cracked up laughing and Aunt Marsha raised her eyebrows at me. Sometimes Mum and Dad get annoyed with me, too, when I talk too long to Mish on the phone. Mum says, "Can't you just wait till you get to school to do all that silly giggling?"

Lucky for Vince, Aunt Marsha went to bed early, too. Otherwise I didn't know how he'd get out to the kennel without her finding out. I don't know how he was sleeping out there but he hadn't complained about it once. He'd complained more about Mandy not being able to come inside. Vince liked to roll around the floor with her in front of the heater and get her to growl when he tried to pull socks out of her mouth. Vince was probably enjoying the kennel and the break it gave him from the kidney and cabbage smell that had taken over the house.

When I went into my room I crossed off another day under the Picasso bird.

APPENDICITIS

E'RE HALFWAY THROUGH NOW. IT'S BEEN THE longest week and a half of my life so far. Longer even than the week and a half I spent in the hospital when I was eight and my appendix burst. Nobody knows the use of the appendix (I did a project on it when I got better). It's a worm-shaped thing that's longer than a pencil and lives in your stomach and it has no job. It's like Uncle Nedley in that way. Except you wouldn't say Uncle Nedley has no use because he has no job. He builds great tree houses, and cracks hilarious jokes, and he makes bread with seeds and raisins when he comes to stay.

But the appendix can't do any of that. It's a mystery to the doctors. Why we have one, I mean. And sometimes appendices (that's how you say more than one appendix) cause real trouble. For no reason at all they become *aggravated*. That's like when your mum says, "Keep it *down,* kids — you're giving me a headache!" Except that the appendices get annoyed without anyone doing anything wrong at all. They're like Mrs. Stills in that way. They get so annoyed that they swell up and up and up until they *burst*. That's what mine did. It burst and whatever was in its guts sprayed into my stomach and I could've *died*. I had to have an operation and go to the hospital for a week and a half. I had a sore tummy and I had to just lie in a bed *all day*. Well, this week and a half with Aunt Marsha seemed to go a lot slower than that whole time lying in bed in the hospital with a sore tummy.

TIME

IDID AN EXPERIMENT ONCE TO SEE IF A KETTLE TOOK LONGER to boil if you actually watched it. It did *seem* to take longer but it was hard to tell because if I wasn't watching it I couldn't tell if it had boiled or not. I asked Vince to help me but he said he was helping Dad in the shed and that it sounded boring anyway.

So far there were eleven red ticks on the calendar — a row and a half. Mum and Dad had been away a row and a half. When I lay in bed at night I counted the days and the hours till they came back. I'd say to myself, *It's Thursday seven-thirty now. That means twenty-four hours till it's seven-thirty Friday.* Then I'd add up all the lots of twenty-four hours till

I got to the time when Mum and Dad got back. I'd close my eyes and I'd still see the days with the red ticks and all the days without red ticks in my mind. I did the same sums over and over in my head and came up with the same answers. I don't know if I was slowing time down or speeding it up but I couldn't seem to stop counting red ticks.

It seemed like when you were around certain people time went faster. Mish was like that, so were the Giannopoulos boys. Dad was like that when he wasn't at work and so was Mum. Other people seemed to make time go slower. Aunt Marsha was more like that. I began to wonder if maybe she had a time-slowing-down power, the way I had telepathic powers with Aidan. Maybe she was slowing down time on purpose. Maybe she'd slow it down until it stopped and we'd be stuck here forever in the middle of the three weeks waiting for Mum and Dad to come back.

LUCKY FOR SCHOOL

LUCKY FOR SCHOOL. WHO WOULD EVER THINK THAT Bettina R. Wendle (R for *Rona* because all the girls in my family have that as their middle name) would be saying "lucky for school"?

For one thing I didn't have to worry about Vince and Aidan when I was at school. I didn't even know where they were because the Grade Sixes are in a different block from all the other kids. And I got to see Mish, and I had to think about things like how to spell *unanimous* and *rhinoceros* and what 24,888 divided by 777 equaled. At lunchtimes I played handball and shouted my head off, and in Art I painted a storm, and Marianne, the guest art teacher, said it was postmodern. I'm not sure what that is but I could tell by the way Marianne smiled at me that it was something very good. Marianne had a tattoo of a turtle on her shoulder. Maybe I'll be like Marianne when I grow up. I'll definitely get a tattoo. I think I'll get a picture of the Picasso bird with the leaf in its beak.

I was getting in trouble from Mrs. Stills a lot. It seemed I got in trouble with Mrs. Stills without even trying. It just happened, usually for giggling with Mish and disturbing the class. But because I got most things right in class she couldn't get too mad. And she was very pleased with how much homework I was doing at the moment. Mrs. Stills didn't know she had Aunt Marsha to thank for that.

Aidan was starting to have a lot more temper tantrums, mostly over Aunt Marsha trying to make him read things other than his comics and eat more than just toast and peanut butter. Vince was getting ruder, too. The little rude things he used to say loud enough only for me to hear, he was starting to say loud enough for Aunt Marsha to hear. "This stuff smells like *garbage!*" he'd whisper when Aunt Marsha put one of her made-up dishes on the dining room table. "What was that, Vincent? Do you have something you'd like to share with the family?" Aunt Marsha would ask. He'd just go quiet then and say, "No, Aunt Marsha," and look at whatever was on his plate.

I was just about finished with *The Lion, the Witch and the Wardrobe* and that made me feel sad, too. I felt like I was going to say good-bye to all these new friends I'd made in the book. Aunt Marsha might make me read a book by Dickens. I'd seen one she was reading lying on the kitchen table. It was called *Hard Times* and it had rain clouds and an empty paddock and a gray house on the cover. It didn't look that good. I cheered up when Miss Fulworth, the school librarian, told me there was a whole Narnia series.

POSTCARDS FROM PARIS

THE BEST THING TO HAPPEN IN THE WEEK AND A HALF WAS that two postcards came from Mum and Dad from Paris. The funny thing was that they both arrived on the same day, even though Aunt Marsha said they were sent on different days. "That's the French postal service for you!" she said.

The postcards from Mum and Dad said that they were having a lot of fun in Paris. They said that they'd been up a river called the Seine in a boat, Dad had eaten snails and he was going to cook them for us when he got back so could we please start collecting, and Mum was getting around in red shoes she'd bought for way too much money in a Paris shop.

They said that they'd taken a lot of photos and that Dad was getting fat from all the bread and butter and jam and that they'd seen a real Picasso painting like the ones on my calendar and could we please put some more money in their bank accounts. That last bit was a joke, because Mum and Dad knew that Aidan, Vince, and me only had forty-five dollars and fifty cents between us and that probably wouldn't go far in Paris.

We had a fight over where the postcards were going to be put up because we all wanted to have them in our rooms. Aunt Marsha said, "Well, children, there's only one way to be fair about this — the postcards will stay in the kitchen so that we are all free to read them whenever we want to." I knew that was the most sensible thing to do but I secretly agreed with Aidan when he stamped his foot and said, "*It's not fair!*" I wanted to put one next to my bed so I could look at it when I was falling asleep. Maybe it would stop me doing so many *How much longer till Mum and Dad get back?* sums in my head.

THE SHAPE OF THE HOUSE

I HAVE LIVED IN THIS HOUSE MY WHOLE LIFE. I KNOW EVERY bit of this house. I know which stair has the rubbed-thin carpet, I know where Vince's finger painting on the wall is (Mum put a couch there to hide it). I know where the scratches on the floor are because of when we rode around the house in a shopping cart when Mum and Dad were next door helping Boris Rivik in his garden, I know where everything is kept and stored and hidden. I know which windows are the jammers and which ones slide open easy as anything. I even know how many steps from the bathroom to my bedroom and from the kitchen to the living room and from the back door to the garden shed because me and Mish played a counting game once and I wrote down all the steps it took.

But now it's like a different house. When I come home from school it smells different and *feels* different. Things are mostly still in the same place but it feels like we're living in a different house — like the *shape* of the house has changed.

AUNT MARSHA'S JOGS

AUNT MARSHA GOES ON A LOT OF JOGS, AT LEAST I think that's what she's doing. She disappears off to the park wearing different-colored tracksuits. There's the black-and-lime-green one, and the orange-and-red one, and the purple-and-yellow one with the stars down the legs, and the all-white one, and the silver one with the gold stripes across the back. She comes back from the jogs with a red face saying, "Ahh, exercise is a tonic for the soul!" Mandy comes back looking tired.

MANDY

MANDY ISN'T BEING MANDYISH. SHE JUST LIES IN HER kennel on Vince's blankets and things all day. We take her for walks and Aunt Marsha takes her on her jogs but she isn't the same. She goes along but more like because she has to than because she really wants to. Aunt Marsha puts her on the leash and Mandy hates the leash. I can understand why — it wouldn't be too much fun if every time you tried to explore an interesting smell or chase after another dog you just met, you got a tug around the neck and someone in a green-and-black tracksuit said "*Heel!*" Mandy spends a lot of time standing at the back door wanting to come inside. I feel like saying, *Don't worry, Mandy — it's probably more fun out there in the kennel.*

HATING AUNT MARSHA

IT WAS THE SECOND SATURDAY WITHOUT MUM AND DAD. Outside it was windy and gray and cold. The weather lady said a big storm was on the way later in the afternoon. Next door we could hear the Giannopouloses playing soccer. Aunt Marsha said this morning was school project day and that she didn't want us getting caught in a nasty storm.

Vince and me and Aidan were sitting on the floor of the boys' room doing our homework. Everything was quiet except for the wind blowing the trees around outside. Until Aidan spoke, that is. "I hate Aunt Marsha," he said, his voice cutting through the quiet of the room.

"I hate her more," said Vince.

"I hate her *more!*" said Aidan.

"You couldn't hate her more than me," said Vince. "I hate her to *eternity.*"

I knew I should have told the boys not to speak about Aunt Marsha that way, that it was wrong and that it was mean and that Aunt Marsha was very kind to come all the way from Canberra to look after us. I knew that's what I should've said. "I hate her more than both of you, *so!*" I said instead, "*Shut up!*"

Vince and Aidan looked at me with shocked faces and the room went back to quiet except for our noisy hating thoughts and the wind bashing against the windows.

UNCLE PAVLOS MAKES A VISIT

THERE WAS A KNOCK AT THE FRONT DOOR. IT WAS UNCLE Pavlos. Even though he wasn't our uncle, Stella said he would like it if we called him that because it reminded him he had family, which was important for a man whose wife had left fifteen years ago for the mechanic. He was usually pretty loud and shouted a lot when he played soccer but when he saw Aunt Marsha he went all quiet for a minute and just stood there and stared.

"What can I do for you?" Aunt Marsha asked.

"Excuse me, Mrs. Marshy," he said. Vince and me giggled when he called her that. His accent sometimes made it a bit hard to understand him. "I have come to get the soccer ball back."

"The name is *Ms.* Wendle," said Aunt Marsha, sounding like the Queen again. (*Ms.* is what you call yourself when you don't want to be *Miss* because it sounds too much like a silly girl and you can't be *Mrs.* because you aren't married, Dad told me ages ago.) "And, yes, you can have your ball back," said *Ms.* Wendle. "Vincent, fetch the ball for Mr. — Mr. —"

"Pavlos! Please call me Pavlos!" Uncle Pavlos said with a smile that was bigger even than the smile he did when he scored a goal. He didn't run round with his shirt over his head though like he did when he got a goal either. I don't know what Aunt Marsha would say if he did that. Uncle Pavlos's chest was like a woolly gray carpet.

"Vincent, fetch Paulo's ball for him, please!"

Even though Aunt Marsha got Pavlos's name wrong he still stood there beaming at her. Vince ran and got the ball and we went back to our school projects. Vince was really playing Nintendo and I was really drawing pictures of the kind of tattoo I might like to get one day. I could hear an argument starting up downstairs.

THE ARGUMENT

"**I** DON'T WANT TO READ ANYTHING NEW, I WANT TO READ *Phantom and the Insect Invasion*! Where are my comics?" Aidan and Aunt Marsha were fighting again.

"You have been reading the same rubbish since I arrived. *Variety is the spice of life*, Aidan. You are going to read something different today!"

"No! I want *Phantom and the Insect Invasion*! Where's my *Phantom* comic?" Aidan screamed back. I thought I'd better go downstairs and try to calm him down.

"It's time for you to read something different from those ridiculous comics!"

"Give me back my *Phantom*! Where's my *Phantom*?" Aidan was shouting now.

"Aunt Marsha, maybe you should give him back his comics. . . ." I said. Nobody ever touched Aidan's comics. Once Vince did and Aidan bit him. That was the only time Aidan ever bit anybody and he got in a lot of trouble for it. Vince made a big fuss and said he'd need a tetmus shot. Dad said, "It's teta*nus* shot, Vince, and don't be ridiculous — you only need that with rusty nails and dogs." Then he gave Vince a Band-Aid and said, "Go and play outside and don't touch Aidan's comics."

"Bettina, stay out of this for once!" Aunt Marsha snapped at me.

"I want my comics! It's not fair!" Aidan kept shouting.

"I told you, *no*!" Aunt Marsha grabbed Aidan's arm. Uh-oh.

"*It's not fair!*" Aidan's voice was splitting my ears. Vince came running downstairs. "It's not fair!" Aidan screamed again and again and then he did the thing I was most scared he was going to do. He bit Aunt Marsha. He bit her on the arm. She screamed and dropped his hand. "*Ooooh, you little devil!*"

Aidan was already running through the back door and out into the garden. Aunt Marsha raced after him with me and Vince just behind her. We saw Aidan climbing as fast as he could up into the tree house.

"No, Aidan! You are not to go up there! Come down at once!" Aunt Marsha called up to him. She had already said that we were not to go up into the tree house while Mum and Dad were away and that she was going to talk to them about having the tree house taken down altogether because it was "ridiculously unsafe."

We knew that Aunt Marsha would never climb up and get him herself. Heights were her One Great Fear.

"That naughty, *naughty* little boy!" Aunt Marsha shook her head. "Come down from there at once, young man! *Come down, I tell you!*" Aunt Marsha stood at the bottom of the tree-house tree and yelled up at Aidan. There was no answer. Aidan knew he was safe. He'd watched *Getaway* with us that night.

Aunt Marsha looked at Aidan's little teeth marks in her arm.

"It's OK, Aunt Marsha, you won't need a tetmus shot," said Vince. I think he was trying to be helpful. "That's only for rusty nails and dogs."

"Vincent, I am perfectly aware of the uses of the tetanus shot. Now . . . Now, g — go up there." Aunt Marsha looked up at the tree-house tree. "And tell your brother to come down at once!" She looked scared.

"He won't come down if he doesn't want to, Aunt Marsha," I tried to tell her. "Sometimes he spends hours up there."

"But that's when he has his comics to read," said Vince. He wasn't meaning to be rude but Aunt Marsha took it that way.

"Vincent, I told you to go up that tree and get him *this instant!*" I'd never seen Aunt Marsha look so upset. The hair was coming out of the basket-shaped bun on her head and her face was turning red.

"Go on, Vince," I said, "try and get him to come down." Aunt Marsha and me watched as Vince climbed up the tree.

"Oh dear, oh my dear, be careful! Please Vincent, be careful." She had the same look on her face as when the lady on *Getaway* skydived off the big cliff.

"Are you OK, Aunt Marsha?" I asked.

"What? All right? Yes, yes, of course I'm all right! Of course I am! But, but we must get Aidan out of the tree. . . ."

"Oh don't worry about him. He loves it up in that tree house," I told her.

"The tree house is unsafe, Bettina. It is *too high*. Your Uncle Nedley and your father built it *too high!*" I didn't tell Aunt Marsha that's what made it the best tree house in the world.

Soon Vince came climbing back down. "He won't come down, Aunt Marsha. He says he's going to stay up there till Mum and Dad get back."

"But he can't stay up there." Aunt Marsha was looking sick now. "A storm is coming!"

I noticed then that a light rain was starting to fall. "I'll go up, Aunt Marsha," I said. "Don't worry, Uncle Nedley built a roof, so he won't get wet."

"Oh dear, oh no, oh do be careful, Bettina, please be careful!" Aunt Marsha called behind me as I started to climb the ladder. When I pulled myself into the tree house I saw Aidan sitting in the corner under the kitchen sink and the shelves. "I'm not coming down," he said.

"Come on, Aidan, please come down."

"No! I'm staying here!"

"Aidan, Aunt Marsha is worried because a storm's coming. Please come down. She won't be mad. She said she'll give you back your comics." I know she didn't exactly *say* that, but the truth was I was getting a tiny bit worried about the storm, too. Aunt Marsha's scaredness was catching on to me. I'd never been scared about the tree house before but I was now. It was so windy and it was starting to sway just a little bit. I really wanted Aidan to come down.

"I'm not coming down, Tine, and you can't make me!"

"What if Aunt Marsha gave you your comics back — would you come down then?"

"She chucked 'em out."

"What? How do you know?" I didn't think even Aunt Marsha would do that.

"I just know."

"I'll go and find out," I said. By the time I got back to the ground my hair was wet from the rain. It was falling more heavily now and I was starting to feel cold.

Aunt Marsha looked terrified. "Bettina, you've got to get him down! He must come down! The wind is getting very strong!" It was true the wind was blowing hard around our ears now.

"Aunt Marsha," I said, "Aidan might come down if he sees that you'll give him back his comics."

"I — I can't give them back, I — I — threw them away!"

I couldn't believe it. Vince gasped behind me.

"But — but, Aunt Marsha, are they in the trash?"

"No, no," she wailed, "the garbageman has taken them away! Oh dear, I'm afraid I have done something terrible . . . something *unforgivable*. . . ."

Vince and me didn't know what to say — Aunt Marsha *had* done something terrible. Suddenly lightning flashed through the sky. Seconds later there was a loud rumble of thunder. The rain began to fall more and more heavily on our heads. "Oh dear, oh no! We shall have to call the police. That's all there is to it!"

"What can the police do?" Vince asked. "They only have guns."

"Oh dear, guns . . . Oh no, we don't need *them*." Aunt Marsha looked even more worried.

"Not unless you want to shoot him down." I think Vince was trying to help.

"Oh dear, oh no, surely the police will know what to —"

"We have to call a fire engine. They carry ladders," said Vince.

Suddenly there was another crash of thunder that sounded very close. I jumped.

"Aaaaaahhhh!" Aunt Marsha screamed like she did when she was watching the *Getaway* show but about ten times louder. "Quickly! Everybody inside! We'll call the police *and* a fire engine!"

We raced inside. The radio was saying how the biggest storm in years was about to hit and that everyone should try to go inside for cover. Even Vince looked worried now.

I passed Aunt Marsha the phone from off the wall.

The first time she tried to dial the number she dropped the phone. "*Blast!*" she said. I'd never heard Aunt Marsha say that before. I think she was swearing and it made me nervous. She dialed the number again.

"Hello . . . Yes . . . Is this the police? . . . I've got a boy up a tree. . . . No, no, I didn't put him up the tree. . . . Well, I suppose I did in a way. . . . Oh dear . . . I am perfectly calm. . . . Yes . . . He's up a tree in a tree house. . . . It's very high. . . . I'm afraid the wind could send the whole thing toppling down. . . . Or the lightning might hit . . . It sounds so close. . . . Yes . . . My nephew says we need the fire engine. . . . Yes, for the ladders . . . No no, they're in Paris. . . . Well, they wanted to renew their vows. . . . I tell you I am *perfectly calm*. . . . How long? Oh dear, all right then . . . Yes, it's 1 Maclusky Street, Baywood. . . . Oh hurry! Please hurry!" Aunt Marsha hung up the phone. "They're on the way," she said.

"The police or a fire engine?" asked Vince.

"Oh dear, oh, I don't know — both I think." Aunt Marsha twisted her hands together and paced up and down the kitchen. Her face wasn't red anymore — it was white. Half her hair had come out of the bun thing and she had big black marks under her eyes from where the rain had half washed her eye makeup off.

"Are you all right, Aunt Marsha?" I asked her. I didn't know what to say or do. "Would you like a cup of tea?" I asked. I think that's what Mum would have said if she was here now.

"No, no . . . You two stay here. I'm going back out to the tree in case he comes down. . . ."

CRASH! There was another roll of thunder, the loudest so far. "We'll come with you, Aunt Marsha," said Vince. Aunt Marsha was already rushing out into the garden and into the pouring rain.

The sky kept flashing with lightning. It was as if the world had turned angry and all the anger was pouring down into our little garden and flashing over us, frightening us, making us small. "Aidan! Aidan!" Aunt Marsha screamed up into the tree again. I'm sure he couldn't hear. The wind and the rain and the thunder were making too much noise.

I could see the whole tree swaying and creaking and all its branches waving in the wind. I felt really scared then, looking at the tree moving like that. I'd never seen it do that before and I'd read a bit about what could happen if you were hit by lightning. "Aidan!" I shouted up the tree. "Ads!"

"Ads," Vince shouted, "don't go under the sink — metal is a conductor!"

"What are you talking about, Vince?" I asked.

"Metal's a *conductor,* Tine. Lightning flashes right through it and then if you touch the metal it flashes right through you and lights you up like a giant *torch* and then you disappear forever!"

"Aidan! Stay away from the sink!" I yelled up. Aunt Marsha was walking around the base of the tree, checking the ladder, touching the wooden rungs, looking up into the branches.

"Oh dear, they've been over fifteen minutes already!" Aunt Marsha checked her watch. "They must have so many calls coming through for help because of the storm. . . . Oh dear . . . I can't leave him up there. . . . Tine" — she'd never called me that before — "could you go and tell the neighbors, the Gia, Gia —"

"The Giannopouloses." Vince helped her out.

"Yes, can you go and tell the Giannapouloses we need their help?" That was the first time I'd ever heard Aunt Marsha say the name right.

"They're not home tonight, Aunt Marsha," I told her. I happened to know that the whole Giannopoulos family was at a wedding because I'd seen Stella out front earlier and she'd told me that Sam had spilled tomato juice all over the front of her best dress and now what was she going to wear to the wedding tonight?

"Aunt Marsha, they're not home," I told her. "They've gone to a wedding."

"That's it, then!" she said. "I shall have to climb up and bring him down myself!"

AUNT MARSHA CLIMBS THE TREE

"**B**UT AUNT MARSHA," I SAID, "WHAT ABOUT YOUR ONE Great Fear? . . ."

Aunt Marsha looked at me for a moment without saying a word, then reached for the ladder. She did the sign of the cross as she heaved herself up. "God protect me," I heard her whisper.

I looked at the flashing sky turning darker every minute and did a prayer, too. *Dear God, please help Aunt Marsha get Aidan out of the tree without anyone turning into a torch.*

Aunt Marsha pulled herself slowly up to the second rung, and then to the third . . . and onto the fourth. Vince and me watched Aunt Marsha's bum in her skirt as it went up the ladder. I don't think anybody with a bum that big and wearing a skirt had ever gone up to the tree house before. I don't think any grown-ups had been up since Uncle Nedley and Dad built it. Was the ladder going to be strong enough? The rungs had always been a bit loose and they were getting looser. I wished the fire engine would hurry up and get here.

"Careful, Aunt Marsha!" Vince called up to her.

"Aaaaah!" Aunt Marsha screamed and her foot kicked away at nothing as one of the rungs came loose. It bumped its way down through the branches to land at our feet. Vince and me looked at each other through the darkness and the thunder rumbled again.

"Aunt Marsha, are you all right?" Vince called.

"Oh dear, oh yes, yes, I think so!" we heard her call back. She must have reached the next rung. She was getting harder to see as she moved higher up into the leafy branches.

Aunt Marsha was almost at the top of the ladder now. I could just see her two white legs coming out from under the branches. By now we were getting drenched by the heavy rain. It must have been cold but I couldn't feel it anymore.

All I could think of was Aunt Marsha and Aidan and how something terrible was going to happen right here in my life right now. I knew the trickiest bit for Aunt Marsha was still to come.

"What — what do I do now?" she screamed down at us. "The ladder's run out!"

"Reach out for the big branch on the left!" I called up. "The one with the butterfly chimes!"

"What?" Aunt Marsha shouted back down.

"The big branch on the left!" Vince called out. "Reach out for the branch on the left!" He turned to me. "Tine, I don't know if she can do it, I don't know if she's going to be all right!" He looked very upset.

"It'll be OK, Vinny. She's very fit — remember all those jogs she goes on."

Suddenly there was a huge gust of wind followed by another loud rumble of thunder.

"Aaaaaaaaahhhh!" Aunt Marsha screamed again as a branch tore away from the tree and came crashing down. Vince and me jumped back as it knocked smaller branches and leaves and bark to the ground. It was as if something was trying to rip the tree apart, branch by branch. I saw the rainbow butterflies from the chimes hanging from the branch and one of Aunt Marsha's shoes caught up in the chimes. "*Aunt Marsha!*" I screamed as loud as I could up to the tree house.

There was no reply.

AN IDEA

"**I**S AUNT MARSHA ALL RIGHT?" SUDDENLY AIDAN WAS
standing beside us!

"Aidan, what happened?" I asked him.

"I climbed down the other side when I heard Aunt Marsha
calling out!"

"What other side?"

"Chris and me have a secret way. . . . Tine, is Aunt Marsha
really up there?"

"I — I don't know what to do." I really didn't. I was the
big sister and I didn't know what to do next.

Suddenly we heard Aunt Marsha calling out. "Help!

Help! I can't move! Help! Help! Aaaaaahhh!" Aunt Marsha screamed the same way she did when she was hanging over the lookout with her head under the fence. I wished Dad was here.

"Tine, what about we use The Mandy Lift to get her down?" said Vince.

"What?"

"The Mandy Lift! Couldn't we use The Mandy Lift to get Aunt Marsha down the tree?"

"But — but do you think it could hold her?" I asked.

"It's pretty strong, Tine. I think it could do the job!"

"But I don't know if it's safe. . . ."

"Come on, Tine, we haven't got much time — the storm's getting worse!"

"All right then . . ." It had been a long time since we'd used The Mandy Lift. Mum said, "Just take it *down!*" but Dad never did.

"Hold on, Aunt Marsha! Don't let go! We're coming!" Vince shouted up. There was no answer from Aunt Marsha.

"I'll get some hay bales from the shed to put around the tree in case she falls!" shouted Aidan. The hay bales were heavy but I'd seen Aidan help Dad drag them around before.

"Quickly then, Aidan! Come on, Tine! We'll climb up the other side and get Aunt Marsha into The Mandy Lift!"

Vince took the harness from its branch and put it over his shoulder.

AUNT MARSHA AND THE MANDY LIFT

THERE WAS NOTHING THAT SECRET ABOUT AIDAN'S WAY OF getting up the tree. It was just the side without the ladder. You had to grab on to branches and pull yourself up. Even though we were drenched and the wind was making the branches sway and shake, Vince and me climbed faster than we ever had.

We were level with Aunt Marsha now. I could see that she was gripping on to the floor of the tree house with one hand and on to the tree with the other while her two feet were on the branch on the right. She was so close to the house she could have pulled herself up. "Aunt Marsha, are you all right?" I called to her through the rain.

Aunt Marsha clung to the tree, her eyes tightly shut as she pressed her cheek into the bark. I reached out and touched her shoulder. She was shaking under my hand. "Oooooh," she moaned, her voice muffled by the tree, "I — I — I can't move, help me, please help me. . . ."

"We're going to get you down, Aunt Marsha, you've just got to do what we tell you. We're going to get The Mandy Lift around you. . . ." Vince shouted.

"Wh — what?" she called back.

"The Mandy Lift, it's how we get Man — oh it doesn't matter, just do what we say, Aunt Marsha, you've got to do what we tell you."

"Oh please, please don't let me fall," she cried.

The tree was moving in the heavy winds — lightning flashed over and over but there was no time to worry about what might happen.

"We won't let you fall, Aunt Marsha," said Vince, swinging around to the other side of her with the harness. "We're going to strap you into The Mandy Lift now, Aunt Marsha." Aunt Marsha didn't say anything. She just groaned like she was sick.

"Vince, Vince, I don't think, I don't know if this is going

to work. . . ." I wanted to cry. I had never felt so scared before. I didn't think I could do it. I just wanted to let go of the tree and be out of the storm and back with Mum and Dad.

"Tine, take the other side of the harness and help me strap her in." Vince's voice sounded strong, the way Dad's did when he told us what to do when we were helping him in the shop. I just had to do what Vince told me and everything would be all right. It was Vince in charge now. I breathed in. "OK, Vince!" I shouted back.

Vince threw the rope to me and with one of us on either side of Aunt Marsha we began to strap her into The Mandy Lift. I could feel Aunt Marsha shaking when I touched her. She was pressing so hard into the tree it was hard to get the straps around her body. My fingers were cold and stiff and it was hard to tie the knots and do up the buckles. Vince had to swing round and help with my side. He spoke to Aunt Marsha in the same soft voice Dad used when we had nightmares. "It's going to be all right, Aunt Marsha," he said as he tightened the harness around Aunt Marsha's back and under her bum. Except for her shaking, Aunt Marsha didn't move at all.

"That's it, Tine, she's in!"

"Now what?"

"We get back down to the ground and let the rope out like we do with Mandy! Quick, I'm not sure how long this branch is going to hold!"

"Aunt Marsha, you have to let go of the tree when we tell you to, OK?" Vince said to her.

"No, no, I can't let go! P — p — please don't make me let go. . . . Please, I'll fall. . . ."

"You have to do what we say, Aunt Marsha. You have to." Vince sounded as sure as Aunt Marsha did when she told us that Mandy couldn't come inside anymore.

"Y — y — yes, all right, *do what you say* . . . All right then . . ."

"Quick, Tine, let's get back down!"

Vince and me flew down the tree. Two or three of the rungs on the ladder came free as we climbed but it didn't matter. Aidan was waiting for us with the hay spread all around the bottom of the tree.

"OK now," said Vince, "it's going to take all three of us letting the rope out to get Aunt Marsha down and we have to let go of the rope slowly." We all took hold of the rope that was dangling down and was attached to the rope harness around Aunt Marsha.

"Aunt Marsha!" Vince shouted up. "We've got you now! You have to let go of the tree!" We waited to feel the pull on the end of the rope, but it stayed loose.

"Aunt Marsha!" Vince tried again. "Let go of the tree!"

"Let go! Let go of the tree!" Aidan and me shouted up. The rope was still loose. Aunt Marsha wasn't going to let go of the tree.

"It's noisy up there! We'll all three have to shout at the same time," said Vince, "on the count of three. *One — two — three!*"

"*Let go of the tree!*" the three of us shouted up together.

Suddenly the rope pulled tight in our hands. "She's let go!" said Vince. "Hold tight!" The three of us held on to the rope as tightly as we could, letting it out slowly, bit by bit. Aunt Marsha was a lot heavier than Mandy. It took all our strength to keep hold of the rope. We could see Aunt Marsha's bum swinging and bumping against the branches in The Mandy Lift as it came down the tree.

She was only a meter or so from the bottom now and the rope was getting harder and harder to hold on to. It was burning in our hands as we strained and pulled as hard as we could against it. Suddenly the rope slipped out of our grip but the safety catch didn't work — as I tightened my grip I felt myself yanked off the ground and pulled up into the air. I looked down — Vince and Aidan hung beneath me as Aunt Marsha dropped onto the hay spread out on the ground. We dangled there a moment, me at the top, Vince in the middle, and Aidan on the bottom.

"Let go of the rope, everybody, on the count of three!" Vince shouted. I think if he hadn't, the three of us might have hung there like that forever.

"*One, two, three!*" we counted together before letting go. Three wet Wendles landed in a heap on the hay beside Aunt Marsha.

A WET HUDDLE

"**A**IDAN! ARE YOU OK? IS EVERYBODY ALL RIGHT?" VINCE and Aidan sat up slowly beside me.

Aunt Marsha wasn't moving.

"Aunt Marsha, Aunt Marsha! Are you OK?" Aidan started to cry. We heard a groan coming from Aunt Marsha.

"Oooh, aaahh."

"It's OK, Aunt Marsha, you're safe, you're on the ground!" I said to her.

"Vince, help me undo these straps!" Vince and me undid the straps of The Mandy Lift with shaking fingers. When Aunt Marsha was free of the rope harness she grabbed on to us tight. She was crying. I felt her body against me. It was hot and cold at the same time, and shaking. I could smell her perfume and her skin and feel her wet cheek against mine. She was crushing me into Vince and I could smell him, too, and feel him wet and shaking and Aidan was pressed into my back and I could feel his bony shoulder in my ribs. We sat there in a wet huddle while the storm raged over us with Mandy jumping round us and whining and licking our skin and Aunt Marsha sobbing and saying words we couldn't really hear.

AUNT MARSHA ON A STRETCHER

"WHAT'S HAPPENED HERE, THEN? IS ANYBODY hurt?" It was the fire engine man.

"Our Aunt Marsha was stuck up the tree," said Aidan, only it sounded more like "*rraunt was shtuck up th tre*" because his cheek was pressed so hard into Aunt Marsha's bosoms.

"Right, then! Stand back and we'll see if she's all right!" We tried to stand back but Aunt Marsha was holding on to us too tight.

"Everything's going to be fine," said another one of the fire engine men. "You're safe now." He pulled us out of Aunt Marsha's grip. "Are you hurt?" he asked her, looking into her eyes. Aunt Marsha was still crying too much to talk.

"She's got no broken bones," said one of the men, checking over Aunt Marsha's legs and arms. "She's just in shock. We'll need to get her inside and out of the cold." They carried a stretcher out of the fire engine and laid it next to where Aunt Marsha was sitting on the hay.

"No, no need for that . . . I think I'm — I'm fine, really, I'm . . ." Aunt Marsha sniffed.

"You've had a nasty shock, madam. We'd better carry you inside, if that's all right by you of course. . . ."

"Oh, oh dear, all right then . . ."

The fire engine men lifted Aunt Marsha carefully onto the stretcher and carried her inside.

"She's going to be fine, kids," said the ambulance man, coming out of Aunt Marsha's room. "She just needs a good night's sleep and some time to recover from the shock. She told me what happened. You children were very brave doing what you did. She's a lucky lady."

I think we felt guilty when the man said that. If it hadn't been for us, Aunt Marsha would never have got stuck up the tree in the first place. If it hadn't been for us, Aunt Marsha would never have had to come down from Canberra and look after us at all. The way Vince and Aidan were looking at the ground, I think they were thinking the same thing as me.

That night we didn't bother with dinner. None of us felt like eating. We didn't feel like doing anything. We didn't turn on the telly or make toast or have an argument, or ring anybody up or play a game of cards — we just sat at the kitchen table doing nothing. When it got to seven o'clock I said maybe we should go to bed. The boys both said yes without a fight.

That night we all slept inside, including Mandy. A branch had fallen on the kennel and made a hole in the roof. Vince made a bed for her in the laundry room in case Aunt Marsha woke up in the middle of the night and found her on the couch or on Vince's bed. I don't think he wanted Aunt Marsha getting any more upset than she already was.

Before we went to bed, Vince and me opened Aunt Marsha's door to make sure she was all right and didn't need anything. The bedside light was on but Aunt Marsha was asleep. Her hair hung all over the pillow and over the side of the bed. I'd only ever seen Aunt Marsha's hair up in that bun thing — I never knew she had long hair. It made her look like she did in the photo we have of her playing with Dad when they were growing up.

"Good night, Vince," I whispered when we were at the door to his room.

"What are we going to tell Mum and Dad, Tine?" Vince looked worried.

"What's *Aunt Marsha* going to tell Mum and Dad, you mean."

"Probably that we tried to kill her."

"But we didn't," I said.

"Yeah but, Tine, she could've fallen out of the tree. . . ."

"But she didn't!"

"No, she didn't." Neither of us spoke for a minute.

"Do you know how scared of heights Aunt Marsha is, Vince?"

"Very scared."

"She really tried to climb the tree and rescue Aidan."

"I know, Tine."

"It was a good idea to use The Mandy Lift," I said, after a bit.

"Thanks, Tine. 'Night."

I said good night and went into my room. I put my yellow moon-and-star pajamas on, then I lay in bed and looked at the calendar and the Picasso painting of the bird with the leaf in its beak. I looked at the rows of red ticks and I thought about Aunt Marsha lying in bed with her long hair over the pillow.

When at last I fell asleep I dreamed the tree house tore away from the tree and me and Vince and Aidan and Aunt Marsha and Mandy went floating through the sky and we saw the Picasso bird with the leaf in its beak.

THE MORNING AFTER

WHEN I WENT DOWNSTAIRS IN THE MORNING AIDAN was sitting at the kitchen table reading a book.

"What are you reading?" I asked him.

"A book," he said, not looking up at me.

"I can see that, Aidan, but I've never seen you looking at a book like that before. What is it?"

"Aunt Marsha's book. By Dick — Dick . . ."

"Dickens."

"Yeah," he said, "him."

"What's it called?"

"I don't know. I can't read the name. It's too long." He

looked up at me. "Is Aunt Marsha going to be all right, Tine?" He looked scared.

"I think so," I said to him.

"But, Tine, if she isn't, will I go to jail?" He had the about-to-cry look. I was feeling as worried as he was but I couldn't show it. I mean, I knew we wouldn't go to jail, but maybe Aunt Marsha could *sue* Mum and Dad if she'd hurt herself. Suing is when you get so mad because someone has done something mean to you that you ask for a lot of money to make you feel better. Uncle Nedley told me because he'd tried to sue the man who'd hurt his knee in the car accident. Mum and Dad didn't have any spare money to make Aunt Marsha feel better and Vince, Aidan, and I only had forty-five dollars and fifty cents between us. The Expensive Monster would tear the house apart.

Mum and Dad would be really mad, mostly with me because I'm the oldest and Dad asked me specially to look after the boys and be good for Aunt Marsha.

"Aidan," I said, "there's no way you're going to jail. Help me squeeze some of these grapefruits for Aunt Marsha."

"OK. I think there's some leftover Kidney Pie in the

fridge. Maybe we could bring some of that to Aunt Marsha for her breakfast."

"Good idea."

While Aidan and me were getting the breakfast tray ready for Aunt Marsha, Vince came into the kitchen.

"What are you doing?"

"Making breakfast for Aunt Marsha," said Aidan.

"Can I help?" asked Vince.

"Yeah, you can make the tea," I said to him.

When everything was ready and the pie was hot from the microwave we carried it upstairs on the tray to Aunt Marsha. Vince even put a flower from the back garden on it like Dad does for Mum on her birthday. I knocked on the door.

"Come in," Aunt Marsha answered.

"We — we thought you might like some breakfast, Aunt Marsha," I said from the doorway.

"It's Kidney Pie," said Aidan.

Aunt Marsha pulled herself up in the bed. She looked different without her bun or her orange lipstick lips or the green stuff she puts over her eyes. And she was wearing pink pajamas. "Ooh . . . ouch," she said as she sat up.

"Are you all right, Aunt Marsha?"

"Just a few bruises, I think." She smiled a bit.

We put the tray down on Aunt Marsha's bed. She looked down at it and then all of a sudden she started crying. It couldn't have been the Kidney Pie, even though looking at it made me want to cry sometimes. Tears ran out of her eyes and down her nose and cheeks and into her hair. She was almost as loud as Vince when he got going. Vince didn't cry much but when he did we all knew about it.

"Please don't cry, Aunt Marsha. We're — we're very, very sorry," I said.

"You children . . ." she sobbed. "You children — you — you — you *rescued me!*"

Next it was Aidan's turn to cry. Then Aunt Marsha did something we'd never seen her do before. She grabbed Aidan and she hugged him. The tray of grapefruit juice and Kidney Pie went spilling everywhere. Little rivers of green grapefruit juice dribbled over the blanket as Aunt Marsha held on to Aidan and he held on to her.

I couldn't stop the big fight that was going on in my throat that means I'm going to cry. I'd managed to stop it ever since Mum and Dad told us they were going to Paris, I'd stopped it at the airport, I'd stopped it when I couldn't put Mum and Dad's postcard in my room, and I'd stopped it when we were tying Aunt Marsha into The Mandy Lift but I couldn't stop it now. It came out in one big sob. Aunt Marsha let go of Aidan and took my hand and gave it a squeeze. "You do such a good job with your brothers, Tina," she said. I was sobbing now. Aunt Marsha looked so warm and nice and big in her pink pajamas with her long hair. Suddenly she was hugging me and kissing my head and the big river of bad news rushed out of me and the fight in my throat stopped and I felt better than I had ever since Mum and Dad first gave us the news.

Vince was standing back when Aunt Marsha took his hand and looked at him. "Vince, you were very, very brave yesterday," she said. "Thank you for getting me out of the tree the way you did."

"That's all right, Aunt Marsha," he said, stepping toward the bed. Aunt Marsha put her fingers through his hair exactly the same way Dad does to him sometimes. He looked pretty pleased with himself.

"Do you want us to bring you another breakfast, Aunt Marsha?" Aidan asked. He was up sitting on her bed now. He had Kidney Pie on his knees. Just then Mandy jumped up on the bed. She dropped Aunt Marsha's brown shoe on the bed — the one she'd been wearing in the tree — and then she began eating the Kidney Pie off the blanket.

"At least someone likes my Kidney Pie!" said Aunt Marsha, and everybody laughed.

"You know I think maybe I'll just sleep a little more, then perhaps I'll have something a bit later. . . . Will you children be all right? Can you make yourselves some breakfast?"

"We'll be all right, Aunt Marsha," I said.

As we were walking out the door, Aunt Marsha said, "I always wanted kids like you," she said.

"You do have us," said Aidan, and we left Aunt Marsha to sleep.

SLOW BIRDS

WE STOOD ON THE BACK PORCH IN THE BRIGHT sunshine with Aunt Marsha and looked at the damage the storm had left behind in the garden. A branch from the tree had knocked down part of the fence between our house and the Giannopouloses'. Another branch had knocked a hole in the roof of the kennel and become tangled up in Dad's thermal sleeping bag. White socks and tea towels and pillowcases from off the line lay all over the grass and hung in tree branches and over the fence. The Mandy Lift lay in a tangle under the tree on the hay. The whole garden was covered in hay and leaves. The breeze blew the hay and leaves up into the air in swirls. "I love the way a storm washes the world clean!" said Aunt Marsha, stepping onto the grass in her bare feet. The breeze blew her hair around her face as she lifted her arms in the air as if they were two wings.

"What are you doing, Aunt Marsha?" Aidan asked.

"Tai Chi!" she said, doing a slow twirl. "It's better than jogging!"

"But we thought you liked to go jogging," said Vince.

"Oh never — jogging's for soldiers or football players. Tai Chi is movement for the spirit!" answered Aunt Marsha, lifting one foot in the air and stretching her arms out in front of her. She looked like a big tall bird in slow motion.

So that's what Aunt Marsha had been doing when she went to the park every afternoon. I wondered if there were more things about Aunt Marsha that we didn't know.

Aidan leaped off the back porch and began to copy her. Two slow birds together. I couldn't resist. Me and Vince and Aunt Marsha did Tai Chi and break dancing and ballet all around the garden with the damage from the storm all around us and the breeze blowing us and the sun on our faces.

THE LAST FOUR DAYS

IN THE LAST FOUR DAYS I'VE TAUGHT AUNT MARSHA HOW TO make tomato soup and spaghetti and she taught us how to do real Tai Chi. We learned the stork and the bubbling well and the floating flower. Vince kept break-dancing instead of doing Tai Chi and Aunt Marsha said maybe we could invent a new Tai Chi move for him called Floating Break-Dancer.

Mish came over after school and stayed for dinner. When she found out Aunt Marsha used to be a children's nurse she nearly fell off her chair. Mish wants to be a children's nurse or an acrobat when she grows up. She asked questions all night like, "Is there really such a thing as an earwig that can crawl in your ear and eat your brain?" and "Did you ever have any kids from the circus in your hospital?"

Aunt Marsha explained how these days she was more and more interested in something called *alternative medicine*, where you use things from the garden, like lavender and roses, to make you feel better. She said if there were kids from the circus in her hospital now she'd probably tell them to make sure they had The Mandy Lift handy when they did those high-flying trapeze acts.

We saw a lot of the Giannopouloses, especially Uncle Pavlos. Every time Aunt Marsha came into a room he stared at her a lot and smiled this smile that he never does for any of us. Aunt Marsha even played a game of soccer with the Giannopouloses because our team was one short. She was goalie and we couldn't get the ball past her. Uncle Pavlos asked if she had played for Australia. She said, "Yes — *and we beat Greece!*" and kicked the ball right past him.

Aunt Marsha took Aidan to Baywood Plaza and they came back with some new comics and *Oliver Twist*, the book. *Oliver!* is Aidan's favorite movie because of the singing and because Mum said he looks like the kid in the film. Aunt Marsha told him Dickens wrote the story and now she reads it to him at nights. Aunt Marsha sang while she swept the hay off the porch, "*When I see someone rich, both my thumbs start to itch, just to find some piece of mind,*" and Aidan finished off with "*You've got to pick a pocket or two. . . .*" It's a song from the *Oliver!* movie. Aunt Marsha told Aidan he was "a gifted child." Vince rolled his eyes at me.

Vince is sleeping in his own bed again. Aunt Marsha and him made a bed for Mandy in the laundry, since the kennel's now got a hole in the roof from the storm. Mandy seems to like it in the laundry. I think it's because she can bring her bones in from outside and chew them in bed. I saw Aunt Marsha patting Mandy in the kitchen and giving her a fresh chop bone and saying, "Thank you, Miss Puppy Dog." I guess in a way Mandy helped to save Aunt Marsha, too, since it was The Mandy Lift that we used to get her out of the tree. And Mandy *did* bring back the missing shoe.

At school I looked up the Eiffel Tower on the Internet. Eiffel isn't the French word for "awful." It's the name of the man who designed the tower — Gustav Eiffel. Gustav Eiffel believed that anything was possible, including building the tallest tower in the world, sending secret messages through the air, and going ballooning. The tower looked tall and beautiful. I read how there was a three-colored light hidden up in the top in the bell tower that lit up Paris. It sounded like just the place where lost romance might be. I was glad Mum and Dad gave it a visit.

In a minute we're going to pick them up from the airport. We're taking Dad's car so everyone can come, "even if it's a squash," Aunt Marsha said. Before I left my room I stopped to look at the Picasso bird on my calendar. Four days have gone by without red ticks — I must've forgotten — and now Mum and Dad are almost home.

"Tine! Come on! Let's go! The plane will be landing any minute!"

"Coming, Aunt Marsha!" I shouted back, and raced downstairs.